I0819560

✦

ALSO BY ANNA-MARIE McLEMORE

Flawless Girls
Venom & Vow (with Elliott McLemore)
Self-Made Boys
Lakelore
The Mirror Season
Dark and Deepest Red
Blanca & Roja
Wild Beauty
When the Moon Was Ours
The Weight of Feathers

✦

Anna-Marie McLemore

WE COULD BE ANYONE

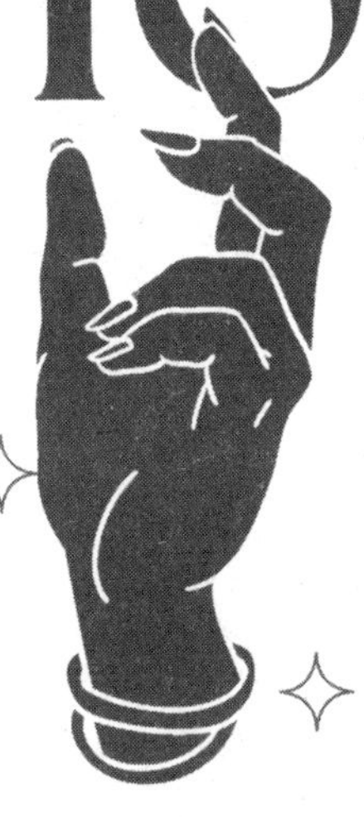

FEIWEL AND FRIENDS
New York

A Feiwel and Friends Book
An imprint of Macmillan Publishing Group, LLC
120 Broadway, New York, NY 10271 • fiercereads.com

EU representative: Macmillan Publishers Ireland Ltd, 1st Floor, The Liffey Trust Centre, 117–126 Sheriff Street Upper, Dublin 1, D01 YC43

Our books may be purchased in bulk for specialty retail/wholesale, literacy, corporate/premium, educational, and subscription box use. Please contact MacmillanSpecialMarkets@macmillan.com.

Library of Congress Cataloging-in-Publication Data is available.

First edition, 2026
Book design by L. Whitt
Feiwel and Friends logo designed by Filomena Tuosto
Printed in the United States of America

ISBN 978-1-250-37058-7
10 9 8 7 6 5 4 3 2 1

FOR KAT BRZOZOWSKI:

You described our process perfectly when you talked about how we follow story breadcrumbs together. Thank you for wisdom along the way, humor that makes the path more fun, and every time you've stuck with a book while we found the magic in the middle of the forest.

LOLA

I KNEW WHY people came to The Coterie.

They came for discretion. No photographs or photographers were allowed up here except for a few times a season, and only with the express permission of the resort's hosts.

They came for luxury. The sheets were fine enough that film actresses swore they prevented wrinkles. Original paintings by Goya or Gainsborough lined even the most infrequently used hallways. Rumor had it that the women bathed in champagne and the men polished their boots with it.

Perhaps most of all, they came so they could lord it over everyone else; an invitation here was so coveted that they could spend the rest of the season twisting the knife. *But I suppose you had to be there.* Or, *Oh, but I've already said too much. We really like to keep things private up there.* Or, *I wish you'd been there to see it yourself.*

Then there was me, the uninvited guest. I was here for revenge.

Papá always thought I had no patience. *You don't know*

how to wait for anything, mija, he would say with a laugh as I stared at frost-covered ground, annoyed that the first flowers weren't yet breaking through. Or when I walked around tripping in a secondhand dress because I wanted to wear it right away, not wait for Mamá to hem it.

I wished they could see me now.

I'd learned the truth about The Coterie months ago, and ever since, my rage had been growing into a living thing, ravenous inside me. I knew if I didn't do something, it would eat me alive. But it had to be the right something. It had to be perfect.

My revenge would be a work of art.

So I'd been coming here for weeks, preparing one detail at a time, like polished knives set out on a lace tablecloth.

I danced past the stained-glass panels on the lower floor, quickly and gracefully enough that anyone inside would wonder if they really saw that strange silhouette crossing the windows.

I sprinkled perfume along the thresholds, a scent that was sweet and out of fashion. Today's socialites swanned around in clouds of rose or violet. None of them were wearing anything like this. The spiced vanilla would call up some past era, perfect to suggest a haunting.

I hid in the bushes and reached out a hand as a woman passed by. As soon as my cold fingers grazed her neck, she ran screaming across the gardens. Once she'd calmed herself, I could see her wondering if she'd imagined the whole thing.

And thanks to the resort's hurried construction, I even found a few places where I could pry the trim of a window away from its casing. Not enough to be obvious. Just enough to let in a few chilling drafts.

When it came to fake hauntings, I was an expert. By the time I was finished, no one at The Coterie would be able to sleep. We'd be able to get anything we wanted out of the owner. Bixby Fairfax may have owned half the movie studios in Hollywood and half the newspapers on the West Coast. He may have been able to bring down politicians with a well-placed phone call. He may have had a silver-screen beauty on his arm. But none of that would stop me from bleeding him dry.

The sun was just beginning to outline the hills in amber, my cue to leave the resort. Hauntings were best faked in the blue hours. Broad daylight had a way of bleaching the mystery and intrigue out of everything.

I did have one more stop to make, through a side door and into a quiet hallway. Detours into the main building were always risky, but I needed something I could pawn. Fast enough to replace the car fare I had secretly borrowed from my brother early this morning.

The Coterie was so cluttered with precious objects that Fairfax stored half of them in the attics, still in their shipping crates. As long as I avoided the central foyer, I could keep from being seen, and I could take a souvenir without anyone being the wiser. I'd done it many times before. My brother's last birthday present had been a book so beautiful it would've been a crime not to give it a more loving home.

I listened for anyone approaching. I watched for ladies setting out on early morning walks, their satin hats as round and colorful as macarons. Nothing. So I surveyed my target:

a credenza so recently polished it smelled of lemon and oil. I considered its offerings. A geometrically patterned amphora. Too heavy. A gilt-embroidered tapestry fragment. Too bulky, too hard to take down from the wall (and too bad, because that was a lot of gold thread).

My favorite finds were the little statuettes I could pocket in one motion. Last time, I'd picked up an alabaster swan that fetched enough to cover my car fare and then some. I wasn't seeing anything like that here, though.

I did like the look of a silver picture frame. It had a nice weight to it, enough to command a good price. Currently, it displayed a photograph of Bixby Fairfax and Blythe Bell, lord and lady of The Coterie. There were dozens of photos of the two of them around here. No one would miss it. No one ever missed anything I took. I scanned every newspaper my brother bought, and there was never once a mention of theft at the hilltop resort.

"A fine piece," the man at the pawnshop said later that morning. He handed over less than it was worth, and we both knew it. But he didn't complain about where I got my goods, so I didn't complain about his prices.

I was almost to the door when he called out, "Don't you want the photograph?"

The back of my neck went cold. I could have sworn I removed the picture of Fairfax and Blythe Bell. Even Stan couldn't look the other way if he thought I was stealing from the most powerful couple on the West Coast.

But no. The picture was still folded up in my pocket.

Stan was alongside me now. He had removed what I thought had been a plain white backing. But he turned it over, revealing another photograph. It showed a sprawling tree and a handful of socialites lounging on its boughs. Their painted lips caught the light. The fabric and beading of their evening gowns dripped from the branches like glittering water.

"Of course." I took the photograph. "Thank you."

None of the women lounging in that tree were Blythe Bell. None of them looked famous or familiar. But they were exactly the kind of lovely, careless women who reveled in The Coterie's glamour and in their own beauty. They glowed with ease and leisure. To them, the resort was nothing but a fairyland. And that was exactly what called to the rage inside me. It was as sharp as fingernails digging into my ankles. It was as strong as hands gripping my calves, holding me to the dusty ground behind the pawnshop.

As I rushed home, the feeling only came on stronger. It stung and burned along my calves. One minute, it was as sharp and focused as an ant's bite. The next, it was dull and spreading, like a growing pain.

When I got back to our rented room, I tore off my stockings.

Twisting cords of dark red entwined my ankles and my lower calves. They looked so much like blood that I touched them to see if they would come off on my hands. But the dark red wasn't liquid. Those lines were raised, like vines clinging to my skin. When I tried to pull on them, the pain was as sharp as trying to rip out my own hair.

These weren't vines climbing up my legs. They were growing out of me, as though my veins were now on the outside of my skin.

When I'd found out the truth about The Coterie, I thought my rage would eat me alive.

But now it was turning me inside out.

LISANDRO

IT DIDN'T START with how he looked. It never did.

Maybe that was why it had taken me so long to figure out I was gay. The things that drew me to other boys were so small and strange that it was easy to write them off. The pronunciation of a certain word, *library* or *mischievous* or *February*. How a scar on his forehead buckled when he laughed.

Or, right now, in the middle of Harrison's Hardwares, the way the boy down the aisle was biting his nails.

I'd always thought of nail biting as a nervous habit. It was exactly why I'd broken it myself, because of what it might give away. But this boy bit at his thumbnail so casually and quickly, with such efficiency, that it made him seem tougher, impenetrable.

Before I realized I was gay, I'd assumed this heat in the center of my chest was envy, that whatever interested me in another boy was something I wished I had. I knew better now. It was something more dangerous than envy.

Lola and I grew up hearing that we could become anything,

but our parents hadn't meant it the way gringo parents did. They meant it as a warning. In the myths they read us, arrogant men were transformed into oysters or woodpeckers. Soldiers who failed at their guard posts became roosters. Young women talked and talked until they turned into buzzing flies (though Lola called that one a bullshit myth meant to shut girls up; Mamá did not correct her).

When our parents told us anything was possible, they weren't flinging open the doors of the world for us. They were telling us to watch ourselves. Propose a dancing contest that you then lose? You might find yourself turned into a tree. Steal a ship and then use it to greedy ends? Look forward to your masts twisting into sea serpents and the sound of the ocean becoming the maddening noise of a thousand flutes played shrilly and out of tune.

Ever since I'd realized what I was, I'd kept on my guard. Especially since the smallest thing—a marble rolled across the back of a hand, the breath hitching inside a laugh—could turn me into a lovesick version of myself.

I refocused on my task, sizing up the jars of tiny magnets in front of me. I weighed the flat disks in my palms, trying to figure out which were best suited for the effect Lola and I wanted.

"What do you do with those?"

I had refocused so hard that I hadn't noticed the boy coming up next to me.

"Some kind of science project?" He reached into one of the jars, his jagged thumbnail white against the dark metal.

"Something like that," I said.

The way he smiled at me was as clear as light through still water. He'd seen me looking and hadn't minded.

But every time someone passed along the end of the aisle, I could feel the bristling static of them watching. A woman pressed her lips together in a pursed smile that was not unfriendly, but a little too knowing. Then came a sneer from a man young enough that I wouldn't have called him *sir* but old enough that he probably expected me to.

A constellation of names throbbed in my temples. Cydon and Clytius, who fell in battle against Aeneas. Nisus and Euryalus, soldiers slain during a night raid because the moon gleamed off the polished metal of a stolen helmet, alerting enemy horsemen. Hylas, adored by Heracles but dragged underwater by naiads, never to be found by his frantic lover.

Any story I knew about two men in love did not end well. When boys like me fell in love, we tempted fate. Whenever I lingered too long over the shadow of another boy's eyelashes on his cheek or the way he pressed his lips together after he said hello, I tempted fate. Especially in a small town.

Especially as a brown boy in a small town.

My panic was a handful of magnets pulling in more magnets. It repelled me out of that aisle without another word to the boy with the bitten-down thumbnail.

I had to get out of here fast. I had to get out from under the looks of everyone who seemed to know what kind of boy I was.

But I took the corner of the aisle too fast. I ran right into the man who'd been staring at us a minute before.

"Watch it." He shoved me hard enough that I stumbled into a display of watering cans. They tumbled down in an echoing clatter.

I crouched to gather them back together. But the cans hadn't even settled by the time the store owner had me by the back of the collar. "You think my morning's so dull I need boys like you bringing your fights in here?"

No such words for the man who'd shoved me in the first place. There never were. Any protest in me was so familiar and so worn down it no longer had distinct edges.

I had to get out of places like this. But then I'd been saying that since I was twelve, and here I still was. Lola and I were small-time thieves. We were lucky to be making it in towns that barely showed up on maps.

"I don't want to see you in my store again." The owner pushed me toward the door. "We don't stock trouble here."

I stumbled onto the sidewalk. "What do I do when I need to buy something?" I asked, because this was the only hardware store for miles, and because apparently I felt like pressing my luck.

"Send that sister of yours," he said. "She knows how to behave with a little decorum. She could teach you a thing or two."

LOLA

OUR PARENTS TAUGHT us that we could become anything if we were clever about it. In the stories they told, sisters eluded hunters by taking the form of doves and then stars. Purehearted boys who let nothing shake their loyalty became mountains. Girls transformed into ocelots to exact revenge on merciless rulers.

But this was different.

This was vines growing out of my body. As I stared at them, tiny green buds dotted their length, the start of new leaves.

I knew this story. I'd grown up hearing it half a dozen ways. A girl offended a king. A maiden defied a goddess. A nymph spurned a prince. So many stories had the same ending: A girl did something wrong and was transformed into a tree for it.

I was letting my anger get the better of me, and it was showing up on my skin. If I couldn't keep it in check, I'd end up another one of those stories, another one of those girls. If I couldn't keep it in check, I couldn't go near The Coterie.

The brass doorknob rattled.

"I'm indecent!" I shouted.

"Sorry," Lisandro said from the other side of the door.

I pulled my stockings back on and settled myself in front of the mirror. "You may enter."

The door opened slowly. By the time my brother came all the way in, I was practicing my expressions in the mirror, perfecting my early Sarah Bernhardt. I never let my expressions get stale. We had a job to do, and my brother would know something was wrong if I was anything but my meticulous, theatrical best.

Lisandro's collar was lopsided, his hair askew.

I caught his eye in the mirror. "What happened to you?"

"A special on watering cans," he said. "Harrison sends his regards. Wants you to know what a proper lady he thinks you are."

"If he thinks sweet talk is going to get me to go out with that horrid son of his"—I reached for my hairpins—"he's going to be sorely disappointed." I pinned a curl in place, trying to stop my fingers from trembling. I tried to make my hands do the normal things they did before our performances.

Lisandro sat on his bed, the coverlet crinkling underneath him. Hotels that were cheap and trying to look expensive always chose the oddest fabrics.

"Guess Harrison doesn't know about your bar fights," Lisandro said.

"I do not get into bar fights," I said. "I simply defend my reputation."

"Defend your reputation?" Lisandro asked. "Is that what you call fisticuffs with a hatmaker?"

"She said my dress was a fake copy of a Parisian design."

"Wasn't it?"

"Yes, but it was a good one." I pointed my eyeliner stick at my brother's reflection. "No one could tell the difference. She only meant to start something."

"And she succeeded." Lisandro flopped back onto the bed. "You know, you don't have to attend every argument you're invited to."

"But it seems rude not to at least RSVP," I said. Then I saw the opening, how to turn the conversation back on him. The less he paid attention to me right now, the better. "And anyway, I do this for you."

"Pretending you're old enough to be in a barroom and getting into altercations with tourists is for me?" he asked.

"I thought we might find you a friend." We'd had enough variations on this conversation for him to know that *friend* meant *boyfriend*. I'd understood how he noticed other boys long before he did.

"I don't need a friend." Lisandro's voice had a heavy sound that made me think he was closing his eyes.

"Are you sure?" I asked. "You seem a little lonely."

"I'm not lonely." Exasperation roughened his voice. "In fact, I would love to be lonely. I would love to be the kind of lonely that involves staying in and having a quiet evening instead of having to dodge through last-call crowds to make sure you're not breaking a bottle over someone's head."

"A quiet evening?" I combed my eyebrows into place.

"Remind me to get you something nice for your next birthday. Turning a hundred and fifty calls for something really special."

I stitched a loose section of the hem on my skirt, making sure the pennies stayed in place. They were going to add the perfect touch to our grand finale.

Lisandro crossed his arms behind his head. "Where'd you go this morning?"

The question sharpened the prickling along my ankles.

"I went to find the hatmaker and finish the fight," I said. "Obviously."

"I'm going to assume, hope, and pray that you're kidding."

The sharpness wound along my skin like the path of a lightning strike.

"Lisandro?" I asked.

"Yeah?"

I knew I should backpedal. One word too many, and Lisandro would know something was up. But the vines were like fingernails digging into my ankles, and all I wanted was my brother telling me there was nothing to be afraid of. That this was no different than the story Mamá told us about the girl whose reflection climbed out of the mirror, thirsting for blood, until the girl took the reflection's hand and called her by her own name. I wanted my brother to tell me what Papá told us when we were small, that there was a way to fix almost anything as long as you were willing to look for it.

I stared at the floor, the carpet so dulled I couldn't tell if it had started out red or purple. I was too much of a coward to tell Lisandro what I'd done, what I'd kept from him, so all I said was, "You know those myths about trees?"

"You want to narrow it down?" he asked. He sounded half asleep.

"Like Poseidon turning Diopatre's sisters into poplars." I ran a few more stitches around a penny. "Or Daphne turning into a laurel tree."

"What about them?" Lisandro asked.

"Do you think they could've done anything about it?" I asked. "Do you think they could've stopped it?"

"Stopped it how?" Lisandro asked.

Stop being angry, came the whisper inside me. *Your anger can transform you only if it's there to begin with.* And that whisper came with a cruel little laugh, because even that voice inside me knew it was impossible. It was as impossible for me to stop hating The Coterie as it was for Daphne to stop Apollo from chasing her. My rage followed me. I felt its teeth in me when I slept. I felt its fingers on the back of my neck every morning when I woke up.

"Nothing." I snapped my powder compact shut, sealing everything inside.

I fixed my hair so it looked blown by an otherworldly wind. I powdered my lips so they'd seem chapped and cold. My white dress was both opulent and threadbare, a once-splendid gown that seemed worn out by ghostly wandering. A fraying dress, out of fashion and purchased second- or thirdhand, always made for the perfect costume. With a few tricks of a needle and thread, I could make tattered fabric seem spun out of cobwebs.

I turned around in my chair. "How do I look?"

Lisandro propped himself up on his elbows. "You look dead."

I put a modest hand to my mouth. “Oh, stop.”

My brother got to his feet and smoothed out his shirt. “Ready for me to banish you from the corporeal realm?”

“I thought you’d never ask.” I smiled, hoping it didn’t look as forced and brittle as it felt.

LISANDRO

"SO *I* DON'T even get to know your backstory?" I asked.

"When two characters interact," Lola said, "neither of them knows what the other is going to do or say. That's the whole point. That's the magic of it. It'll be more genuine if it's a surprise."

"I'm not a character," I said. "I'm your brother. And the last person you should be surprising."

"And it's the highest compliment I can give you to trust you with my method of verisimilitude," she said.

"If I had any idea how you'd use that acting book against me, I never would have gotten it for you."

For the past week, Lola had been haunting a public garden / private library. Public because even peasants like us were allowed to stroll the landscaped grounds. Private because we would have needed a bribe or a papal writ to handle any of the books, all rare.

In the basement beneath the special collections, we made sure everything was in place.

"You're really wearing that?" Lola eyed my plain tan shirt and plain brown trousers.

"Yes," I said. By being unremarkable, I could get away with almost anything. When you were in our line of work, any scheme could be your last, but if no one remembered you, you had a better chance of making it to the next one.

"You're taking years off my life." Lola thinned her voice to a whisper so it wouldn't echo. "That outfit is so dull it might genuinely kill me."

"Someone's in a mood today," I said.

"I am not."

"And anyway," I said, "I'm not here to draw attention. You are." I was the spiritualist in our act, the young man so thoroughly in connection with the afterlife that I could guide a troubled ghost to the other side. Lola wanted me to be more of a showman, but I preferred to give the impression that I was detached from worldly concerns, up to and including dashing outfits.

"Go greet the mark," Lola said. "I need a moment to immerse myself in my character's psyche."

"Don't forget to put the wires back on your way out," I said. "We want flickering sconces, not an electrical fire."

"Have I ever forgotten?" she asked as she disappeared around a corner.

"Yes," I whispered after her. "You have. And it was dumb luck that the entire chalet didn't go up in smoke."

The gallery level lent itself to a haunting. Portraits of dead men loomed out from the paneled walls. The only windows looked out onto hedges where it was easy to hide our equipment. The antique carpets were heavy enough to add to the atmosphere but not so heavy that carefully placed magnets couldn't lift the corners.

When I heard someone talking, I paused on a staircase landing. I recognized the voice, the director of special collections, the man who'd discreetly hired me.

"It's been frightening to no end," he said.

My sister had that effect on people. She knew how to pop out of the shadows at just the right moment. How to vanish before anyone got too good of a look at her. How to wander through a dimly lit hall in such a way that an observer couldn't be sure whether they were seeing things. When she rounded a corner, she gave the air of escaping into another realm.

"The wives won't even set foot in the building," the director went on.

"They always blame it on their wives, don't they?" A second man laughed. "The husbands can't bring themselves to admit they're just as afraid of monsters under the bed."

"Half of them won't cross the threshold," the director said. "The other half want us to perform public séances, make a spectacle of the whole thing. Neither of those befits the image the family wants for the endowment. They nearly canceled the gala entirely. The only way it went forward was by compromise. A tea out on the lawn. Broad daylight."

By the time I was through, they'd be able to hold midnight concerts in the map room.

"This sort of thing can happen anywhere," the second man said. "There was an old yachting club just up the coast. A situation not unlike this one."

It was a situation exactly like this one.

"They brought in the same medium," the second man said, "and not a single sighting after he did his work."

It was our guarantee. If our clients saw the ghost again, I'd return their payment. Of course, we were never around long enough for anyone to ask for a refund. But why would they? As soon as they paid us, Lola never haunted their halls again.

"He's a little young, isn't he?" the director asked.

"In the realm of ghosts, a hundred years old is young," the second man said. "You can't put an age on these kinds of gifts."

"And he seemed a little strange."

"All the most gifted ones are. In fact, the stranger, the better. It's the oddest ones who have the most powerful knack for this sort of thing. Other mediums will come in, commune with the spirit, but a week later, windows are opening on their own, howling in the attic again. And you've paid for nothing. But this boy, he'll get the job done."

"From what I hear"—the director's tone relaxed into the thrill of gossip—"they could use him up at The Coterie."

My attention sharpened. That couldn't have been our work. We'd never set foot up there. We couldn't have even gotten jobs washing dishes in the second kitchen. Every member of the staff had been hired away from the best hotels in the world.

Some called The Coterie a mansion, but *mansion* was an understatement. It was a sprawling hilltop resort. It was an estate that served as a playground to those who already treated the world as their playground.

"Haven't you almost got to feel sorry for whatever ghost gets stuck around there?" the director said.

"You mean having to look at Fairfax's sour face for all eternity?" the second man asked. "What sin in life could warrant that?"

Under their laughter was a trace of envy. The Coterie was the most exclusive resort on this continent. The only way in was to be a chosen guest of Bixby Fairfax or his lady of the house. Rich men and their wives wanted nothing more than what their money couldn't buy, and no one could buy an invitation to The Coterie.

Which, apparently, had a haunting problem.

If we could pull off a job at The Coterie, our reputation could take us anywhere. Lola could have the grand stage she'd longed for, jobs that paid better in both cash and prestige.

And I'd get to know what it was like to live where there were other boys like me, where we didn't have to hide from one another and everyone else. I'd heard of whole hidden worlds in New York and San Francisco. After-hours gatherings in museums. Apartments where the only second looks you got were if someone was interested. Flower shops with secret doors into spaces where everywhere was at least a little queer.

"Care to stay and see the medium at his work?" the director of special collections asked.

"I'd be delighted," the second man said. "I find this all fascinating." When I met the director in the gallery, he asked if I wouldn't mind the second man looking on.

"Of course," I said, obliging, deferential, though I made a point to show a little self-consciousness, a slight darting of the eyes. I needed both these men to talk about me to all their rich friends, but I couldn't seem too eager to impress. I'd let our show make the impression.

Every detail of our act would strengthen the word of mouth that traveled up the hill to The Coterie. The creaking noises. The flickering lights that then went off entirely. The corners of curtains and rugs that danced as though a windstorm were blowing through the gallery.

And thank goodness for Lola's obsession with costumes. The pennies she'd sewn into her skirt let out a faint, eerie tinkling. Even before she made her entrance, those coins sounded like church bells echoing across centuries.

It all built toward her appearance, the ghost of a heartsick girl. She wailed as she seemed to levitate above the mantel.

The director's friend ran from the room.

My sister made an impeccable ghost. The length of her limbs gave her a spindly quality, as though she were extending a hand through time and space. She knew how to let her hair fall in front of her face in a way that haunted even my nightmares. And the final click of the lock was her eyes. She could keep them open, unblinking, in a way that made her look startled. Haunted. The best way to haunt someone was to seem haunted yourself.

"Leave me be!" she cried through the din of slamming doors and creaking walls.

The director of special collections flew back into a chair.

"I've come to help you, my child," I said, like a reassuring priest.

"You've come to mock me!" she shrieked. "Just as all the guests mocked me!"

For the first time, I noticed the tattered lace streaming off her hair. She'd pinned on an old, torn wedding veil she must have gotten for pennies. She was playing a new character, the jilted bride.

"Just as my own betrothed mocked me!" she said.

"Then he was not worthy of you!" I told her.

The director of special collections gripped the wide arms of the chair. He was almost as unblinking as Lola.

"And now they all run from me!" Lola toiled to new heights of sobbing.

With a subtle adjustment to her posture, Lola gave a little extra motion to her skirts. The pennies chimed louder and more brightly, like distant wedding bells. It was so subtle that the director probably didn't know if he was hearing them or if they had simply been called up in his mind.

"They gaze upon me, and they flee!" Lola cried.

"Do you see me fleeing, my child?" I drew closer to her but not so close that the secret light giving her a blue-green cast would fall on me.

She grew still, taking care to look both hopeful and suspicious. Transfixed yet wary.

Then came my usual speech. The peace she sought was not in this world, but beyond. There was nothing left for her here in this realm. All those who loved her, all those who valued her, waited on the other side.

Lola gave me an eye roll so subtle that the director of special collections couldn't see it from across the room. I knew what that look meant; we'd had this wordless conversation a hundred times. *Get some new material.*

I widened my eyes back at her. *Why fix what isn't broken?*

She returned to character, crying softly and prettily. When she'd delivered her full performance, she gave a delicate sigh, a graceful wave of her hand. With a covert flick of a lantern, she retreated into a veil of indoor fog. (Dry ice—expensive, but it gave an excellent return on investment. Nothing lent atmosphere like mist and the sudden lowering of the temperature in a room.)

Then the jilted bride was gone.

And we had enough to live on for another two weeks.

"Remarkable," the director said as he handed over my fee.

"Lost spirits wish to find their way as much as you wish them on their way," I told him. "They only need a little guidance, just as we all do from time to time."

"I cannot thank you enough," the director said.

"I assure you"—I nodded, imagining the tale of our performance drifting up into the hills—"the honor was mine."

LOLA

"BRAVA." LISANDRO SET a raspberry seltzer in front of me, my usual celebratory drink.

"Why, thank you, kind sir." I lifted the glass in my best imitation of a toast.

But everything reminded me of what I was hiding under my stockings. The twists of metal on the hotel lighting fixtures matched the twisting of the vines. The potted plant across the lobby loomed, an omen of my fate. The salad on a nearby table turned my stomach, as though the leaves of lettuce were my future body, disassembled.

My brother and I ate half our dinners in the hotel bar, where the soup was as cheap as it was oversalted and the lamps were always low enough to hide the threadbare upholstery. But right now, Lisandro seemed so proud it might as well have been Delmonico's.

"That was inspired," he said. "In fact"—he leaned in so he could lower his voice—"don't you think it's time we got you a better venue?"

"What are you talking about?" I asked.

He looked around, as though checking if anyone was listening. No one ever was. Everyone at this hotel was on their way to somewhere else.

"There's supposedly some kind of haunting up at The Coterie," Lisandro said.

I set down my glass. I tried to take hold of my expression. Acting during a job was one thing. Acting in front of the one person who could read every little shift of my eyebrows, every twitch of my nose, was another.

"I heard them talking about it at the library." His dark eyes looked illuminated, like the moon on the ocean at night. "So what do you say we make ourselves the ones to solve it?"

"How?" I coughed out the word.

"What do you mean, how?" he asked. "The same way we always do. We paper enough to get us there. We figure out how to send the recommendation up the hill so they come looking for my services."

I stalled, taking a bite of my Welsh rarebit—melted cheese over bread with a fancy name. Usually my favorite food—why wasn't it everyone's favorite food?—it now tasted like cardboard in my mouth.

"Nothing?" Lisandro asked. "I thought you'd be thrilled. Isn't this what you wanted? We could go anywhere. We could go to New York. You've been talking about Broadway since you were five years old."

"And you've always said we'd need money to get there."

"Well, this is how we make it."

"You always said our act would get lost in a big city. Too much competition. Too many mediums all reaching into the same pockets, remember?"

"Not if we pull this off," Lisandro said. "If we pull off a job at the number-one resort in the country, we'll have enough credibility to challenge any act in any city. With word of mouth, we'll have more referrals than we know what to do with. No more papering. People will come to us."

He was saying what I'd thought so many times. This had been part of my plan. This was why I had gone up there. This was why I had played the mysterious ghost in the bone-white gown, appearing through garden mists.

"We're ready for this," Lisandro said. "We can do this."

I studied the tablecloth, trying to guess where the echoes of old stains had come from. Lavender from red wine. Faint green from steamed spinach. A spot of coffee bleached out to the color of parchment paper.

"I don't know," I said.

"You've never been shy about your talent." Lisandro leaned back. "Why start now?"

This was what I had wanted, to create a problem that Bixby Fairfax would pay us to solve.

But things were different now. I was so angry at Fairfax and The Coterie and its guests that it was turning my veins into vines. If I couldn't even keep my anger locked inside my own body, how could I pull off the most complicated job we'd ever done?

"I was thinking about what you asked me," Lisandro said. "About Diopatre's sisters, about Daphne turning into a tree."

I looked up from the tablecloth.

"And I think they could've fought back," he said. "They could've fought back and kept themselves. But can you blame them for not trying? They were up against gods. And when you're up against gods, you better not start a fight you can't finish. But I know this is a fight we can finish. So are we really letting it go because we're afraid to try?"

Everything brightened at once. Every dim lamp, the fabric on every chair, the shine of every glass. My brother was right. The vines on my ankles weren't a sign that I needed to shy away from this. They were a sign that I needed to finish what I'd started. I'd been right the first time. My anger would eat me alive if I didn't do something with it. And I knew exactly what I needed to do.

The Coterie had decided my fate once. I wasn't letting it happen again.

"Okay," I said.

Lisandro smiled. "Okay?"

"Yeah," I said. "You're right. Let's do it."

That glint in my brother's eyes made me believe anything could happen, even the most wondrous of our parents' stories. A brave horse could become a princess. A princess could become a fox with eyes like the moon shining off dark ice. Those with the purest of hearts could become handfuls of stars or stags who could outrun the dawn.

A brother and a sister could outsmart men who thought they ruled everything.

LOLA

AMATEURS CREATE PROBLEMS.

Experts solve them.

Artists know how to do both.

My brother and I were true artists.

Every night, over our bland dinners—this place was terrified of offending the traveling businessman's palate—we worked out how to put The Coterie under our spell. We mapped out every possibility. Tricks with the windows. Luminous paint. Little bits of ribbon that would look like gray wisps of smoke or green tongues of otherworldly flame.

"Getting the dry ice is still a problem," I said.

"If we get the angle on the lighting right, we might be able to do without it. At least until our finale." Lisandro sketched in the margin of a paper menu. "My question is, how do we get you up there to make your first spectral appearances? We need these vague rumors of a haunting to get more specific."

"You let me worry about that part." I studied his drawings so I wouldn't have to meet his eye. "How about you worry about getting our referral? Who's going to recommend the quiet young man with the wise-beyond-his-years gaze?"

"I was hoping we'd figure out some kind of connection with Fairfax's daughters," Lisandro said. "But that's a dead end."

"Very much so. They don't even live there. The leading rumor is that they can't stand their father's mistress." I leaned in so close that if anyone was looking, they would've thought we were searching for sentient life in our soup. "But I've heard it's juicier than that. I heard they're all living scandalous lives. And do you want to know how they fund them? They extract hefty allowances from their father in exchange for staying out of the public eye and not embarrassing him in polite society."

"Sounds like we're in the wrong business," Lisandro said.

"Doesn't it? I heard one of them even rents a whole villa in Italy. She has a different lover every season. Only lets them stay around until she tires of them. But here's the even better gossip: Fairfax's son. Prevailing lore is that he's troubled. Dangerous. Some even say possessed. Maybe we can get paid for an exorcism."

"First we need a way in," Lisandro said. "My best idea is the dressmaker in town. Blythe Bell herself frequents the shop."

"The one on Carroll Street?" I said. "I know one of the fitters there. She owes me a favor. I got her out of a bad dinner date by rushing in pretending to be a cousin with horrible news."

"I never thought I'd be so grateful that you can't mind your own business," Lisandro said.

When I glanced up, my eyes were drawn to the other side of the hotel's ground floor.

A woman in lavender stood at the reception desk.

"Who's that?" Lisandro asked.

Her gown was layers upon layers of chiffon, the kind so delicate it ripped when beaded by any except the most skillful hands. It was so densely embellished that it made swishing noises as the clusters of beads whispered together. Her hair, the vivid red of ash tree leaves in autumn, was all the brighter against the pale purple.

I had a bad feeling about those colors.

"Do you know her?" Lisandro asked.

"Do you get out from under that rock very often?" I asked. "You don't recognize her?"

Lisandro looked, considering. He had a talent for staring without seeming like he was staring. He appeared to be sitting back, casually taking in the whole scene of the restaurant and lobby. But I could almost hear the gears in his brain grinding on whether we'd done work for her or her family, if she'd been someone's bored young wife or spoiled daughter. There was always the possibility that we would cross paths with previous customers. Though it rarely happened, it did happen. Lisandro made his appearance so unmemorable that most people didn't look at him long enough to recognize him. The one time someone did, I put on such a good show of being the shy, meek little sister that the man and his wife never made the connection between me and the ghost I'd played.

I wished that was how I knew this woman.

"I don't remember her," Lisandro said.

"That's because you haven't met her," I said. "But believe me, you know her."

He started naming films we'd seen in the past few months—"Was she in that one?"—trying to match her face to a story. She had one of those faces that half of actresses seemed to have. Small, upturned nose. Lips as carefully outlined as her eyebrows. And she was the kind of doll white that directors sought out for how it would read on film. I would have needed white stage paint to match her.

"That's the Magnificent Karina," I whispered.

As soon as I said the name, I could see the recognition in Lisandro, dropping straight and fast as a plumb line. He might not have known her face, but he knew her name.

"*That's* the Magnificent Karina?" he asked.

"Unfortunately," I said.

"The Magnificent Karina who claims she drove a ghost out of a governor's mansion?" he asked.

"Sadly, yes," I told him.

"The Magnificent Karina who insists that spirits leave messages in her nail lacquer?"

"Regrettably."

He paused. "The Magnificent Karina who's supposed to be at the service of Midwestern millionaires for the next three months?"

I was right there alongside him.

"Why would a famous medium leave an easy job to visit a county where coyotes outnumber humans?" he asked.

"Now, isn't that the question?" I said.

Some manufacturing scions in Indiana had wanted the Magnificent Karina to clear any and all hauntings from their numerous homes and warehouses. I would've done so many devious things to get us that job.

Yet she had abandoned it.

"How do you even know that's her?" Lisandro asked.

"Because I've seen her pictures," I said. "Don't you ever open a newspaper?"

"Don't I ever . . ." He caught himself raising his voice from a whisper to past normal volume. "Do you think the papers show up in our room by magic? I'm the one buying them."

"Well, you clearly skip the fashion pages," I said, "because that's where I've seen her."

The Magnificent Karina was still at the front desk. She appeared to be examining a map and demanding something.

"She was photographed posing with some couturier," I said. "Supposedly she cleared her new estate of some pioneer woman's malevolent spirit."

"There are so many things wrong with that sentence I don't even know where to begin," Lisandro said.

"There were so many things wrong with their ensembles I don't know where to end," I said. "And that's before getting to the hats."

"People actually stay here?" The Magnificent Karina's voice punctured the air. "They *sleep* here?" Her eyes took a sweeping inventory of the lobby sofas (bits of stuffing poked out at the seams), the floors (badly in need of refinishing), the wallpapers (faded and peeling where the sun had worn away the paste). "Overnight? Truly?"

"We pride ourselves in being the only hotel in the area, mademoiselle," the concierge said.

"First place by default." The Magnificent Karina ran a finger over the reception desk as though checking for dust. "You do have baths here, don't you? I wouldn't even be staying the night except I don't want to arrive at The Coterie smelling of train car."

The ringing in my head grew louder. Not only was this awful woman here; she was here to take what was ours. She was here to cash in on the haunting I had set up.

She was here to step into the middle of a fight I needed to win.

As the Magnificent Karina moved, metal flashed at the hem of her dress.

Constellations of sewn-in pennies.

No, not pennies. They had the matte finish and patina of antique coins, each probably valuable enough to be displayed under glass. Yet there they were, swinging around her embroidered boots, showing off what she could afford to drag over the ground.

My brother was trying to keep his face neutral, but he looked as crestfallen as I was enraged. He had no idea just how much the job at The Coterie meant to me, but I knew what it meant to him. I knew he clipped articles from obscure newspapers about The Dash in San Francisco, the gay hamlets of Fire Island, the social balls that were blurs of lavender and pansy-flower confetti. He wanted out. He wanted to go somewhere he wouldn't worry about getting the shit kicked out of him for smiling back at a guy who smiled at him first.

"We'll figure out another job," he said.

"What are you talking about?" I asked.

"Well, we can't go up there now."

"And why not?" I whispered. "We can still win this. We bring the best show we have, and they'll see that she's a fraud and that we're, you know, better frauds."

"You've done this too long to pretend you don't know how this works. We stay out of the way of anyone who claims to do what we do." Lisandro glanced toward the reception desk. "Too many cooks burn down the whole kitchen."

"So we just let her have it?" I asked. "Why do *we* have to stay out of *her* way?"

"She has a big reputation." Lisandro shrugged and leaned back, his best *c'est-la-vie, que-será-será* posture. As though this gringa coming in and stealing everything from us was nothing. "She doesn't need us to let her have it. The moment she shows up, it's hers."

"But we're better," I said.

"It doesn't matter," he said.

"Bullshit," I said.

"Language," he said.

"Mierda."

I had never met this woman, yet I hated her with the fury of two colliding galaxies.

"We'll find another big job," Lisandro said.

There were no jobs this big, and he knew it. Even if there had been, this was the one we needed. This was the one *I* needed. I wasn't letting myself become one of those stories. I wouldn't be another girl who became a tree, her silence making some king's path a little smoother.

We had a whisper-thin thread of a gold chance, and there was no way I would let the Magnificent Karina snatch it from our hands.

LISANDRO

THAT NIGHT, I dreamed of boys like me. Not ones I'd met. Boys from the myths I'd grown up on.

I dreamed of Carpus, son of the west wind, who fell in love with Calamus, son of a river god. I tried to warn them against their swimming contest (which had always, to me, sounded like a way to distract themselves from how badly they wanted to kiss each other). I tried to warn Carpus of the rogue wave, but he did not hear me, and he drowned. Then Calamus, in his despair, let the water take him, and soon all that was left of their love was the whispering of river reeds.

I dreamed of Hyacinthus, the beautiful prince loved by Apollo. I watched Apollo teach him to shoot a bow (sporting activities seemed to be the preferred way such men either expressed their desire for each other or distracted themselves from it). I called out to them, trying to tell them that Apollo should not teach Hyacinthus how to throw the discus. But they didn't hear me. The discus struck and killed Hyacinthus, and his blood bloomed into the spring flowers that bore his name.

I dreamed of Achilles and Patroclus, Nisus and Euryalus, lovers and soldiers in wartime. I tried to warn them of their fates, but they could not hear me over the clash of metal.

When I woke up, the room was dark. The space felt off-balance, as though the entire building had tilted slightly to one side.

Lola wasn't in her bed.

When I turned on the light, I found makeup scattered across the writing desk as though she'd just used it.

It wasn't the first time my sister had sneaked out. Lola took joy in few things more than sitting in an unassuming corner of a hotel lobby, listening to the gossip of other people's lives. It inspired the characters she played, and it had led to a job more than once.

But this was different. I could feel the wake she'd left in the air. I'd seen the loathing in her eyes earlier that night, and I should have known.

If my sister was doing what I feared she was doing, I needed a plan. So far it consisted of me running down the stairwell, holding Lola's best dress, wearing a hat that hopefully made me look different in case the on-duty night clerk and I had met before.

That was all I had. That, and the hope of a better plan coming together by the time I reached the lobby.

I scanned the ground floor, looking for my sister. She wasn't in any of her usual spots, her favorite worn-out chairs tucked into shadows.

My plan was still distinctly half-baked by the time I went

up to the reception desk. At least I could use how out of breath I was to sell it.

"Has she already checked in?" I asked.

"Pardon?" the night clerk asked.

"I'm sorry." I made a show of getting myself together, smoothing my shirt. "I mean, could you tell me where to find a guest known as the Magnificent Karina?"

Even keeping my head down, I could sense the skepticism in the man's posture.

"Please." I didn't try to mask my desperation. I didn't need to. There were no easier lies to tell than ones you could prop up with the truth of what you really felt. "She requested this dress be waiting for her when she arrived."

I displayed the evidence, a gown that read as pleasantly lilac under hotel lamps but that turned to a sickly purple-gray under ghostly lighting. Lola had meticulously repaired it and lined the inner hem with neat rows of pennies. Not that the night clerk could see the pennies from the way I held it. The weight just made the beading look heavier and richer.

"I fouled up the dates," I said, "and I thought she was arriving tomorrow, so the gown is late, and if I don't grovel enough to make good, she'll have my employer's head, and then he'll have my job."

The longer the night clerk was silent, the more the sweat on the back of my neck chilled.

"Good luck to you," he said in a professionally distant voice.

I looked up just enough to meet his eyes.

"She's been in a horrific mood since she arrived," he said.

"She's asked to be moved three times because the mirrors weren't to her liking. But I believe the lady has deigned to spend the night in room five thirty-one."

Every bit of my breathless thanks was genuine.

I ran back up the stairs, hoping to catch my sister before she got to the door. If I had to pull her off the Magnificent Karina, I'd have to figure out how to persuade the woman not to call for the police. Maybe I could convince her that Lola was possessed? Perhaps she could even banish the evil presence. She could bask in her own skill, and in the marvelous story she would have freshly on hand to tell everyone at The Coterie.

No one was in the hallway. But as I approached 531, I heard the faint echo of my sister's voice.

"You will return whence you came, or else"—Perfect. So Lola was already threatening her. Absolutely perfect.—"suffer the unending consequences."

Inserting myself into this mess was an astonishingly stupid idea. I was a brown boy about to burst into a rich white woman's hotel room in the middle of the night. If I managed to keep my sister and myself out of jail, it would be the greatest trick I had ever pulled off.

I threw open the door.

The image I'd expected—Lola pummeling the Magnificent Karina, the Magnificent Karina screaming or pummeling her back—stood in contrast with the scene before me.

There was no fighting, no fingernails slashing across faces. no pulling of hair. The room was dark, save for the glow from a familiar lantern, one we often used to underlight Lola.

There she was, my sister, a macabre imitation of a ghost.

All her usual subtlety was gone. Fake blood streamed down her cheeks as though she'd cried it. It dripped from one corner of her lips as if she'd just eaten a beating heart. Luminous paint glowed on her skin in threads of pale, unearthly green. And the sudden draft of me throwing the door open blew wind through the ribbons trailing off her sleeves.

A woman had pressed herself up against the opposite wall. She wore a velvet sheath that could have been either a dress or a nightgown. Her face was dewy, free of any makeup, and her hair, long and dark blond, fell to her waist.

I marveled at the magnitude of Lola's mistake. She was frightening an unsuspecting hotel guest half to death.

But if Lola had gotten the wrong room, how had the night clerk sent me to the same one?

Then I saw the copper hair flowing over a wig stand. I saw the gold boxes of powders and colors.

Underneath the fine wig and the careful makeup was the Magnificent Karina. She was fair-haired and soft featured and younger than I would have guessed. She looked nothing like herself.

When the Magnificent Karina saw me, her stricken face broke into a soundless scream. She clutched her pocketbook to her chest, the trailing fringe of sequins and beads trembling in her hands.

I had just added to Lola's tableau. I was a dark figure in the doorway, appearing next to a girl's bloody, reanimated corpse. I had burst onto the set of *Revenge at the Haunted Hotel*, a motion picture directed by and starring Lola Bernal. I was now a nameless extra. Undead Boy in Background.

Lola smiled, teeth bloody. The grin squeezed more fake

blood from the corners of her mouth. She must have hidden a sponge soaked with it under her tongue.

The Magnificent Karina's scream went from soundless to full volume. She grabbed her coat and shoes and dashed out onto the fire escape, leaving everything else behind.

Including my victorious little sister.

LISANDRO

BY THE TIME the door fell shut behind me, the Magnificent Karina had gotten far enough down the fire escape that I couldn't see her.

"What have you done?" I asked.

Lola smiled her fake-bloody smile. "You're welcome."

"I didn't thank you," I said. "I most certainly do not thank you."

"You should." Lola started going through the little boxes on the dressing table. "I just got rid of our competition. This job is as good as ours, like it was always supposed to be. After all, I warned her"—she transitioned into her little ghost girl voice—"of the eternal peril if she does not return to those she has forsaken and finish the work she did promise to do."

I really hated when Lola did the little ghost girl voice. It always sounded as though, if you refused an invitation to her doll's tea party, she might summon a falling church bell to cleave your head open.

"The dead do not appreciate broken promises," Lola said.

In the little ghost girl voice.

"Please stop," I said.

"Friends do not break promises." She was still doing it.

"Seriously. Stop."

"And when we discover that someone is not behaving as a friend to us, that they have broken a promise"—and . . . she was still doing it—"things can become most unpleasant."

Lola shuffled through the Magnificent Karina's cosmetic tins and jewelry boxes.

"Don't do that," I said.

"Why not?" Lola asked.

"She could come back any second," I said. "Let's get out of here."

"She's not coming back," Lola said. "You saw her face. She's halfway to the train station by now. She thinks a hundred temperamental ghosts take her abandonment very personally."

A knock came at the door. "Is everything all right, madam?" The man's voice didn't have the authoritative ring of hotel staff. This was the venturing of another guest, one who was either concerned or curious about the commotion.

"There was a mouse," Lola said loudly enough to send the words through the door.

Except it wasn't her voice. Or the little ghost girl's voice.

It was a disturbingly perfect imitation of the Magnificent Karina's.

"It's gone now, though," she said. "You may go."

"All right." The man sounded slightly annoyed, his chivalry rejected. "Good night, then."

Lola looked even more pleased with herself. She celebrated by draping one of the Magnificent Karina's evening gowns against her own dress.

"What were you thinking?" I asked. "We have rules for a reason."

"And sometimes we make exceptions." She admired herself in the mirror, the green fabric as vivid as a manicured lawn. "What we do is an art form. Sometimes we must adapt our brushes to the palette we have before us."

"With some rules, there are no exceptions. And you know one of them? Never try to con a con artist." I said each word even more slowly than the first time I'd given her this rule, three years ago. Three years ago, she'd understood it. My sister had been more reasonable at thirteen than she was now at sixteen. "It's messy. It's complicated. And if they ever figure it out—which is a lot more likely than with any other mark you could choose—you've made an enemy."

"I disagree." Lola was now looking through the Magnificent Karina's papers. An engagement diary. A small collection of mail. A couple of slim volumes as finely bound as books but that bore no markings on the spines. "The easiest person to con is the one who thinks they're smarter than everyone else. Con artists make perfect marks because they think they can't be conned."

"If this is how you want to work," I said, "we will fail, at this or at any other job."

Lola was now unfolding the Magnificent Karina's mail.

"We can't go behind each other's backs like this," I said.

Lola was giving a letter her rapt attention.

"And," I said, "you're not even listening to me."

Lola looked up, her face stricken.

"What?" I asked.

She handed me the letter.

The paragraphs rushed at me out of order. Postscript at the

bottom. Greeting at the top. A quick skimming of the contents. But it was the signature that halted me.

This was a letter from Blythe Bell, mistress to Bixby Fairfax, lady of the house at The Coterie. She'd signed it with only her first name, and that one word revealed a familiarity between her and the Magnificent Karina.

The Magnificent Karina hadn't just come looking for fame and money. Blythe Bell had invited her. Blythe Bell, the adored starlet, was expecting her and would be sending a car for her in the morning.

Blythe Bell could not thank the Magnificent Karina enough for canceling her previous engagements, for traveling all this way to attend The Coterie's spectral occurrences.

Blythe Bell could not wait to meet the Magnificent Karina.

"They're waiting for her." Lola sank down on the Magnificent Karina's bed. "We never had a chance. They've been waiting for her." With the blood on her face, she looked both vampiric and dejected, as though death itself had disappointed her.

"All that for nothing." Lola surveyed the lantern on the floor, then the ribbons on her dress. Even the gown she'd taken from the Magnificent Karina's wardrobe looked deflated.

Maybe it was Lola holding that dress.

Maybe it was the precise imitation of the Magnificent Karina's voice she'd done a minute ago.

But a lock in my brain clicked open.

"What if it wasn't for nothing?" I asked.

Lola looked up at me.

"We have a problem, that we can't show up as ourselves," I said. "And we have another problem, that if the Magnificent

Karina fails to appear at The Coterie, a lot of powerful people are going to wonder why. So what if she does appear?"

"What are you talking about?" Lola asked.

Maybe I'd been smarter three years ago, too, because I was talking about something I never would have considered at fourteen.

"You were right," I said. "She's not coming back. What would she do, complain to the management about a ghost in her room? That would reveal a bit of a hole in her professional skill set, wouldn't it?"

That almost got a laugh out of my sister. She rubbed her eyes with the sides of her fingers.

"I demand"—she was doing the Magnificent Karina's voice again—"to be moved to less spirit-infested accommodations."

"That." I pointed at her. "You can imitate her so well it's frightening."

"Wait." Her impression fell away. "You're not talking about me pretending to be her?"

"Well, I'm not pretty enough to do it," I said.

"And you want me to do all this in the presence of Blythe Bell?" Lola asked. "How am I supposed to be enough of an actress to not seem like an actress to an actress's face?"

"She's not a very good one," I said. "You saw her last picture."

"You do realize that if I play the Magnificent Karina, you'd have to play the ghost, right?"

"I'm sure I'd figure it out," I said.

"Oh, because it's so easy. Because an actor's work is nothing, really."

"You're the one with the more difficult job here," I said. "You have to pretend to be someone else. Someone alive."

"Isn't that a bit of a flaw in this plan?" she asked. "What happens when word gets back to her that she's supposedly in California when she's actually in the Midwest?"

"That's why we do this right or we don't do it at all," I said. "We take her act. You become her."

Lola's next laugh was louder, disbelieving. "So you didn't want me conning a con artist, but now you want me to steal from her?"

"Look at all this." I gestured at the wardrobe, the dressing table, the wig stand. "She left you everything you need."

"She's been in the society pages," Lola said. "What if someone compares a photo from the paper?"

"Didn't you see her?" I asked. "Without all this, she doesn't look like the Magnificent Karina any more than you do. She creates the Magnificent Karina out of expensive dresses and good wigs and heavy eyeliner. No one's more careful with costuming than you. You don't think you can duplicate what she does? In newsprint, no one would be able to tell the difference."

"And what if she does come back?" Lola asked.

"Let her try," I said. "By the time we get ourselves installed there, she'll look like the imposter, not you. You'll even have that letter. What's she going to do, say a ghost came into her room and stole it?"

Something shifted in Lola's expression. I almost had her.

"If we're swapping parts," she said, "you have to listen to me. You've never been the ghost before. You're going to have to plumb the depths of your soul to pull this off."

"And if we're swapping roles," I said, "you have to listen to *me*. You've never been on the customer-service end of this. You're going to have to plumb the depths of *your* soul to keep your temper in check during polite dinners and endless croquet matches."

"Deal." Lola got to her feet, grabbed my hand, and shook it. "Where do we start?"

Over the next few hours, Lola read the Magnificent Karina's correspondence as though studying lines for a play.

As the sun came up, she selected one of the Magnificent Karina's red wigs, each as shiny and realistic as the hair of a fine doll.

She pinned on a crown of draping pearls, adding to the glamour of her look and anchoring her new head of hair.

She changed into one of the Magnificent Karina's gowns, the one that was so bright green it looked self-illuminated. With the fire red of the wig, she looked as striking as a green wax candle.

My sister had become the Magnificent Karina so much that when she went down to the lobby, the hotel staff cowered. They braced for her next complaint. And they seemed to share a collective sigh when she only smiled and left to meet the waiting car.

LOLA

THE COTERIE LOOKED a little different when you weren't trespassing. Instead of sneaking up a service road, I was seeing it as an invited guest.

As the driver crested the hill, the main building filled the windshield, as large as a strange castle in a fairy-tale illustration. Bell towers pointed toward the clouds. Terraces jutted out on all sides. Heavy balconies transitioned into stone staircases. There were so many of those staircases winding around the outside that it looked like the patterning on a candy cane.

I'd seen all this before, through evening and early morning mist. But now, in full daylight, it looked ridiculous. It was a monument so clearly meant to showcase wealth that it was almost funny, like wearing an entire bridal bouquet as a boutonniere.

The driver pulled through the open gate and onto a wide brick path. It curved in front of a quatrefoil fountain so huge I might have thought it was a swimming pool, but I knew this place well enough to know better. The outdoor swimming pool—I'd heard there was another indoors, reserved for favorite guests—was off the south side of the house. The bright aqua water stretched out as vast as a lake, surrounded by a replica of some ancient temple, complete with columns. And I'd never seen evidence of anyone swimming in it. In these dry hills, that pool was as breathtakingly wasteful as pouring fresh water into the sea.

I was going to have the most wonderful time ruining all of this for everyone.

"I do hope you enjoy your stay, miss," the driver said.

"Oh, I will," I said.

Lisandro was right. We could do this. We could make a fortune that could change our lives.

I hadn't started a fight I couldn't win.

I'd started a fight that could win us everything.

The impossibly tall front doors opened, the bronze embellishments catching the sun. Blythe Bell, a figure I'd seen only on a movie screen, trotted down the white marble steps. Her head of blond curls gleamed like a polished car, and her navy suit was edged with a shock of orange piping.

"You're here!" she sang out, reaching for my hands. "My goodness, you're even younger than you look in your pictures, aren't you?"

I laughed gently. Wisely. "I'm older than I look. It's a peculiarity of my calling. The spirits affect our beings so strongly that depending on what they give or take from us, we can seem a decade younger or older almost overnight."

She drew her hands to her own cheeks as though overnight aging might be contagious. "Oh, how horrible."

Just as on-screen, Blythe's eyelashes were so long and so

thick with mascara that her eyelids seemed sleepy from holding them up. Her penciled eyebrows arched all the way out to her temples, making her look perpetually surprised. Perfect for the ingenue roles in which she specialized. She'd moved away from those lately, though, supposedly at Fairfax's urging and financial backing.

This was the woman for whom Bixby Fairfax had thrown over his wife, for whom he'd alienated his grown daughters, for whom he'd built The Coterie.

This was the woman who now caught me staring up at the spires, so tall they seemed built to pierce the sun.

"Bixby did go a bit overboard, didn't he?" she said with a demurring laugh. "You set out to build a little country house, and before you know it, you have one hundred and ninety rooms."

In the foyer, dark lacquered floors spread out below carved and painted ceilings. Richly patterned carpets covered the central staircases. And it was all cluttered with antique furniture, paintings, tapestries, mounted objects ranging from swords to spoons.

Roughly every tenth frame was a photograph of Fairfax or Blythe or both of them together. Fairfax playing golf. Blythe playing lawn croquet. The two of them on a carriage ride in front of a city hotel. Several larger frames held painted portraits of Fairfax or Blythe, each of them in regal attire. Other portraits showed what I assumed were Fairfax's relatives. Long-dead ones, judging by the suit styles on the men and the shapes of the bustles on the women.

Several paintings—that landscape, that scene in a throne room, that still life with flowers and eggs—looked vaguely famous. Others seemed familiar in a way I couldn't quite place until I took everything in. A good quarter of the paintings seemed to be of objects in the house. An oil portrait of that chair. A watercolor of that lamp. A dramatic pastel rendering of the rug under our feet. It gave a fun house–mirror effect, as though everything here existed in duplicate or triplicate.

"You might find the layout a little confusing at first," Blythe said. "It was built to give everyone the utmost privacy. Every story has its own set of stairs outside as well as in. But it's really very intuitive. Follow the stone balustrades, and you'll never get lost. I'll have someone show you up once your trunks have arrived, but your quickest way to the suite is to take that staircase just out there. Embry!" Blythe called out to a boy passing through an adjacent room. "Embry, come say hello!"

He looked older than I was, maybe a little older than Lisandro. Yet he did as he was told as readily as if he were a child.

Blythe set her hand on his shoulder. "This is Bixby's boy."

His hair was almost as blond and curly as Blythe's, but that was where the resemblance stopped. Blythe's eyes were blue, like Fairfax's (I knew this from a painted portrait at the public gardens / private library). But Embry's were brown, almost as dark as mine and Lisandro's. Those he must have gotten from his mother.

Embry Fairfax, I knew, was the only Fairfax child who could stand his father and his father's mistress enough to live here. But for all the wealth at his disposal, he wasn't putting it to much use. His clothing was almost as forgettable as Lisandro's, the dullest shades of gray and navy.

"This is the Magnificent Karina." Blythe almost whispered

it, as though conveying some delicious secret. "Embry, take our guest's coat."

"Oh, no, thank you," I said.

I never let anyone take my coat. The biggest snobs in the world sweetly offered to take your coat just so they could check the label. To hand over your coat was to hand over your secrets.

"I tend to run colder, especially when acquainting myself with a new space and its presences," I said. "A side effect of being in close connection with the spectral realm."

"Of course," Blythe said. "I hope you won't be too cold in the bell-tower suite. It gets wonderful sun exposure. Some of the best light of any of the rooms."

"You're putting her all the way up there?" Embry asked. "By herself?"

"Why?" I widened my eyes. "Is it haunted?"

Blythe looked startled. Then the joke landed.

"I'm sorry." She laughed. "I must say, I didn't expect someone in your line of work to have much of a sense of humor."

"Oh, you must be able to laugh," I said. "Spirits need levity as much anyone else."

"Really, we didn't mean to put you away from everything." She was worrying at her fingernails now. "I thought you'd want the space. My head of housekeeping said you phoned this morning?"

Yes, I had. I had phoned to say that I required an adjoining suite for my spectral essence.

"It is an unusual request, I understand," I said, "but I do appreciate it."

"Not unusual for around here," Embry said. "We just had a guest demand a second king-size bed for his prized show dog."

Lo and behold, the first discernable glimmer of personality from Embry Fairfax.

"And we've made the note about your meals," Blythe said. "I understand you'd like to take them in your room?"

"For the sake of communing with the spirit. That's why I ask for two plates to be made up at each meal." I was barely lying. The ghost would in fact be the one consuming the other plate. The ghost just wasn't quite as dead as everyone thought. "If I regularly open a space to invite the spirit, to make clear that the spirit is welcome to commune with me, it does help draw them out."

"How fascinating," Blythe said.

Only gringas found such things fascinating. Lisandro and I grew up leaving out pan de muerto and sugared marigolds every autumn with our mother and father. Now we did it for our mother and father.

"I do hope you'll join us for cocktails," Blythe said. "Our bartender makes the most delicious Mary Pickford, the perfect balance of pineapple and grenadine. In fact, she's right in that little room over there. Go and let her create something for you. Relax while we make sure your trunks have come up from the hotel."

As I followed her gestured directions, I heard them talking behind me.

"My father wants to know where he should put the shipment from Venice," Embry asked.

The sound that came out of Blythe was too vehement to be

a sigh. A huff, maybe. "Back on the steamer to Venice, that's where he should put it. If your father keeps buying things, we're going to need a second estate just to store them."

I found the room Blythe had pointed me toward. In the center of the richly decorated space was a wisp of fog. It rose up in delicate curls, like a cloud forming. I followed it, crossing the threshold.

A girl stood behind a polished wood bar, chipping off pieces of dry ice with a metal pick. With gloved hands, she transferred the pieces into glasses.

This was a girl who knew how to style herself. Her dark, pin-straight hair was cut to her chin in the most precise bob I'd ever seen. The ends were as straight and sharp as the rims of the glasses she was lining up on the bar. Her thick eyebrows were groomed but not overly plucked, adding a lushness, an extravagance, to her features. Her outfit was clearly a uniform, but she'd pressed the white shirt and neat black skirt to perfection. A pin-striped vest made the outfit into something daring, a look off a Parisian runway.

I watched her measure out different liquids into glasses of different shapes. Half the bottles she was pouring were liquor, yet she couldn't have been older than my brother. If she'd lied about her age, her skill must have helped sell it. She poured ribbons of green and red as though she were painting. She did everything with such certainty, such authority, that her employer might never have questioned her age.

"Can I get you something?" she asked.

I hadn't realized she'd noticed me. She hadn't looked up once.

There was an edge to her voice, something like annoyance.

I was interrupting some process as delicate as a chemical reaction over an open flame.

When I didn't answer, she did look up. She only half lifted her head, but her eyes met mine.

This wasn't annoyance.

This was suspicion.

I'd never met this girl, but she was watching me like she already had her guard up against me.

Another voice intruded into the room. "So you're the spiritualist I've heard so much about." The man's voice was deep and resonant. It would have sounded almost grandfatherly if it weren't for the note of appraisal, as if I were an item to be picked up off a museum shelf and inspected.

"May I make you something, Mr. Fairfax?" the girl asked.

Fairfax. The name was the searing cold of dry ice against my fingers.

"No, thank you, Hayden," the man said.

I turned around, finding every feature I'd seen before in newsprint. His gray hair was thick and shining, buckling on either side of a sharp middle part like the halves of a book. His morning suit was carefully pressed, his patterned pocket square a silk so expensive it looked liquid. He stood tall, lean, with the posture of a distinguished professor. But unlike most men his age, he wore no spectacles, so I could see that gleam of appraisal in his eyes even more clearly.

This was the man responsible for The Coterie.

This was the man who had taken everything from me and my brother.

"We're looking forward to you giving us all a good show," he said.

I caught the subtle order in those words. This was about spiritualism to Blythe, but to Fairfax, it was about spectacle. It wouldn't do for me simply to banish the ghost. He wanted fanfare, an exhibition to get everyone talking.

I smiled. "Expect nothing less."

LISANDRO

ATTIC SPACES. WINDOWS. Balconies. Terraces. Exterior and interior staircases. The Coterie was a dizzying game of trapdoors, and I had to learn to navigate all of it.

But first I had to get inside without being seen.

It was almost dark, which made finding my way harder but gave me more shadows to work with. I paused on a stone landing, listening for footsteps or voices. The only nearby sound was from a small alcove, where a fountain splashed water from one marble basin to another.

The water looked strange, like molten glass. The surface of the lower basin didn't stir the way it should have. It reflected the lamps as sharply as a mirror, like a translucent sea.

I hovered my hand near the water. I slid my fingers under the stream. The second it hit my hand, my fingers were coated and shining.

Oil. The fountain flowed with clear oil instead of water.

A sound alerted me, like the light scratching of fingernails on brick. I took a cautious look over the stone wall, trying to place the source.

Down in a lower garden, a boy was sitting on a stone bench. He had his head down, and I watched him through tree branches, so I couldn't see his face. In the light of the garden lamps, his hair looked like pale amber. He was holding a book of drawing paper, the shadows of leaves patterning the pages.

With a sweep of his fingers, he sketched the most perfect circle I'd ever seen anyone draw freehand. A shiver of heat spread up from my lower back and across my shoulders, like water drawn up through a tree's roots and out into its branches.

Don't look. It was like a whisper from a hundred myths I'd heard growing up. It was a mythologically bad idea for me to keep looking. I could feel it in that shiver. If I kept watching, this boy would become someone I wanted to watch.

His posture shifted. I realized he was about to look up a half second before he did.

I ducked back behind the staircase wall.

"Is someone there?" I heard his voice from the garden, the texture like the slight grain of the stone under my hands.

I was silent. I did not move.

This was how you stopped a mistake from becoming a disaster. You stayed quiet and still until whatever sound you'd accidentally made, whatever light you'd accidentally shifted, seemed like nothing but a figment of someone else's imagination.

LOLA

THE EVENING COCKTAIL party was so much bustle and glitter that it spilled out of the salon. Even from out in the hall, I caught flashes of it. Men strode around in satin dinner jackets. Ladies sparkled in exquisite gowns. Chandeliers glowed as gold as the champagne glasses. Everyone laughed and roared in conversations that blended together into festive noise.

It was just the distraction I needed.

I walked the halls, a vial of perfume in my palm, sprinkling it at thresholds and onto the edges of rugs. It was the same one I'd been using when I sneaked up here, the smell heavy and sweet and rich. No haunting was so evocative as when you attached a scent to it.

I sealed the perfume vial and slipped it back in my clutch. Then I made my entrance, my orchid chiffon cape trailing behind me.

"Is that the medium? Thank heavens," I heard one of the ladies say to another. "I've been dying of boredom waiting for something to happen around here."

She was dangling her shoe off her foot. I recognized the blown-glass heel. I'd seen it in a catalog. The price tag would have bought Lisandro and me nearly two months at the hotel.

Blythe ushered me over, introducing me to the women around her. "We're so pleased she's come. It's grown so unnerving around here. The sounds. Especially at night."

Of course Blythe was hearing sounds at night. The Coterie had been built so fast it was as porous as a piece of driftwood. Every time I came up against an interior wall, it sounded hollow. Some seemed thin enough that I could have kicked through them.

Blythe had changed from her earlier outfit into a lemon-yellow evening gown that nearly matched her hair. Her coupe glass held a golden cocktail.

"Bee's Knees," she said, lifting the glass toward me. I thought she was giving some kind of toast until she said, "Have you tried it? The most sublime combination of lemon and honey."

Guests milled around pedestals and credenzas. Every room of The Coterie was stuffed with antiques. The salon was crowded not just with sofas and armchairs but with things on every surface and wall. Cabinet paintings. Silver chalices shaped like nautilus shells. Alabaster figurines just like the ones I'd stolen.

"This is all rather exciting, don't you think?" said an older woman in a royal-blue dress.

"Hauntings, mysterious presences," said a woman with an ostrich plume affixed to the side of her head. "It's like a book, isn't it?"

"A gothic horror novel," Blythe said.

"There's no reason to think the worst," I said. "Ghosts are no different than the rest of us. Just like people, some are pricklier than others, so sometimes they must be won over, which takes time, effort, patience, finesse. And some spirits must be drawn out. They might not feel safe to be approached. Some are even more frightened of you than you are of them."

"Well, that's very sad," Blythe said.

"That's exactly how I feel," I said. "So it's my work to make them feel at ease."

The salon sparkled with necklaces and rings. It gleamed with cuff links and perfectly pomaded hair.

And it was buzzing with my arrival. Everyone was looking at me while trying to seem as though they weren't.

Everyone except the baby bartender, who had a cordial smile for every single person in this room but me.

I took a glass of leftover ice from the woman in the royal-blue dress. "May I refresh your drink?"

I brought it over to the bar. "I don't know what she was having. Something green?"

Before I even pointed to the woman, Hayden said, "I've got it." She was already whisking something into such a froth it looked like sea-foam.

Every moment I watched Hayden, I got a better idea of why they'd hired her. She arranged colors and garnishes like she was making little works of art. She did it fast. And she had a phenomenal memory for what everyone was drinking. Even the requests for less vermouth or extra orange peel.

Hayden was clearly a favorite around here. Fairfax even lifted his glass in greeting to her on the way by.

I needed her to warm up to me.

Then the beacon appeared. Shining. Serendipitous. On the credenza behind the bar was a familiar book, covered with a familiar shade of dark blue cloth.

Ovid's *Metamorphoses*. The same edition I'd gotten my brother for his last birthday.

"What do you think?" I asked, as airy as a breeze through an open window.

Hayden added a twirl of honey to the glass. "Of what?"

I pointed toward the credenza. "Ovid?"

"I've read it before."

This girl was as lacquered as the wood of this bar. Nothing got in.

"Do you have a favorite? Wait, let me guess." I leaned on the bar. "The one with Demeter and the gecko. Or maybe the herdsmen who were turned into frogs?"

Hayden slid the glass toward me. "Can I get you something else?"

Again with the conversation-stopping words.

"Have we met before?" I asked.

"I doubt it," Hayden said without looking up.

"Then perhaps you'll understand my confusion about your hostility," I said.

"I don't have to know you." She started mixing a batch of something red with grenadine. "I know your kind. You prey on grieving families by telling them you can contact their loved ones."

I barely kept my Magnificent Karina voice in place as I said,

"I would never do that." They were the truest words I had spoken since arriving. It was one of the first rules Lisandro and I had ever made together. We didn't reach our hands into the pockets of grieving families.

"But you do," Hayden said. "You have. Blythe's not the only one who's read about you." She spun a glass stirrer through the mixture, swirling the colors together. "I know the kinds of tricks you run. In fact, let's see if I have the gift of foresight. I'm guessing any time now you'll be getting a message from someone's dead relative."

She looked up. "How am I doing? Am I getting warm?"

"Believe me when I tell you," I said, pressing down my anger, "you couldn't be more wrong."

"Oh yeah?" A half smile quirked the side of her mouth. "I saw you in the hall. With your little perfume bottle. Nice touch, by the way. I hadn't heard of that one."

My blood went cold enough to freeze the vines under my stockings.

"Look." Hayden leaned in, lowering her voice. "I get it. You want to make money off them. I don't blame you. They throw flowers on the ground when they have parties and trample on them. They polish their boots with champagne. They hired a chef whose sole responsibility is to make sure the yolks are perfectly centered in the fried eggs. I can't fault you for wanting a little of what they have for yourself. It's the way you get it that I hate."

In Hayden's eyes was enough raw contempt to ruin everything.

"You're a fraud." She said it with a smile; our conversation would have looked social to anyone observing. "Worse, you're a cruel fraud. You don't care about anybody. So I may be obliged to serve you drinks, but I'm not obliged to make you think we're friends. I'm not obligated to be impressed with you. And I'm not obligated to buy a single ounce of the horseshit you're trying to sell everyone else."

LOLA

"WE HAVEN'T EVEN figured out how we're making me appear," Lisandro said. "And you want to start now?"

"What's the matter?" I asked. "You were the one who thought playing the ghost would be so easy."

"What happened to our lead-in?" he asked. "Strange noises, mysterious lights, distant voices? You do remember we planned this, right?"

"We don't have time for that." I'd already made a mess of the sitting area in our suite, my things and the Magnificent Karina's things jumbled everywhere. I kept hoping that shuffling it all around would help me think.

Lisandro studied a bottle of Heinz, still sealed. "Why did they give you an entire bottle? How much ketchup does one person possibly need for one meal?"

"Two people, one living, one dead, remember?" I said. "You should see the dining room. Legions of ketchup bottles."

"And why are you wearing your wool stockings?" he asked. "I thought you only wore those in winter. In fact, I distinctly remember you giving Mamá a fashion lecture for even suggesting you wear them on an unseasonably cold spring day."

I was wearing wool stockings because they were the thickest I had, the only ones I trusted to hide the vines on my legs.

"If you haven't noticed, the air in this house is one big draft." I threw one of the Magnificent Karina's beaded scarves out of the way. "Can we please focus on the problem at hand?"

Lisandro caught the scarf before it landed on our dinner plates. "Your bartender is one person." He set it to the side. "And she's not paying our fee. Why do you care?"

"You know how this works," I said. "One raging skeptic, and we're done before we start. We have to convince her."

"Okay." Lisandro was now finishing his dinner fast, like a snake unhinging its jaw. He was still chewing as he got to his feet, wiping his hands on a cloth napkin nice enough that he seemed uncomfortable holding it. "So what do you want us to do?"

"If we're smart about it, we can settle this tonight," I said. "Blythe announced a late alfresco gathering after dinner."

"What the hell does that mean?"

"I don't know," I said. "Card games. More cocktails. Cigars for the men. So my best plan is for us to catch Hayden while she's going back and forth, setting things up for the outdoor bar. Ready for your ghostly debut?"

We got Lisandro into his costume, his usual plain trousers, but with an oversize shirt that I'd pinned and tucked. With my handiwork, it looked like a flowing garment from another century. I put makeup on him and subtle traces of luminous paint, so he'd look made of otherworldly light. And I told him exactly where the evening fog eddied and gathered, giving him the best place to hide and then appear.

He did not ask how I knew that.

"You get into position," I said as I smoothed out the makeup on his forehead. Lisandro wouldn't come close—that was too risky—so this all depended on Hayden having the sight line to notice him when he appeared. "As soon as Hayden is about to pass where we want her to be, I'll approach her. As soon as she stops in the right place, you emerge, okay?"

"You're just going to approach her for a casual chat?" Lisandro asked.

"Oh, there's nothing casual about this," I said. "We have a conversation to finish, and she knows it."

"Can we go back to what I said about you keeping your temper in check?"

"My temper is perfectly in check. My temper is in checkmate. Now let's go."

I waited on a marble bench in the garden, reading my own copy of *Metamorphoses*. With any luck, it would break the ice. But I wasn't counting on it.

As soon as I heard Hayden's sure, punctuated walk on the path, I sat up straighter.

Hayden was going the wrong way.

She wasn't going toward the marble bar that overlooked the pool. She was descending a half flight of steps set into the grass.

Hayden carried half a dozen bottles—one in each hand, two tucked under each arm—to a stone bar I hadn't even known was there.

When Blythe had mentioned midnight card games *on the terrace*, I'd assumed she'd meant the raised marble terrace, the one perched on top of the columns that flanked the pool.

But there were so many terraces here, and I had been

careless to assume Blythe had meant the largest one. Of course, ladies like Blythe would toss off phrases like *on the terrace* and simply assume everyone knew which one they meant. *Why, this terrace—which other could it have been?*

Every other time I'd been up here, I'd been hiding in shadows. But now I could truly look at everything. And I could see just how many places there were for a bartender to serve drinks during The Coterie's unending string of parties. There was a bar tucked into an alcove near a trio of birdbaths. There was a wooden one near the croquet court. And the one where Hayden was setting up now, a stone counter in the lower gardens.

The laurel trees rustled above me. I could almost hear their branches twisting along the garden walls, whispering that if I wanted to take on The Coterie, I'd need to be a little more clever than this.

If I was going to get Hayden in the right position, I had to stop her before she went down those steps again.

"Hayden," I said the next time she was coming from the house.

She looked exhausted by the mere act of laying eyes on me.

"What can I get you?" She had the stems of fluted glasses crossed between her fingers like she was in a handbell choir.

"Nothing," I said.

Hayden went on her way.

"Wait," I called after her.

"I'm working," she said.

I followed her. "I'm not who you think I am."

I hadn't realized the words had been on my tongue until I'd said them.

They were far too close to the truth.

I trotted after Hayden, the Magnificent Karina's stiff, un-broken-in shoes pinching my feet. "Will you listen for one minute?"

"Unless you want me to pour you something, no." Hayden stopped, turning around to look at me with that open scorn I'd seen earlier. "And you know what—even if you do, I'm not set up yet. Everyone's still at dinner; I don't know why you're not in there with them."

The laurel trees stirred above us. The movement sharpened the stinging along my calves, as though the trees were clawing at the vines under my stockings.

I wanted to grab Hayden's arm and pull her where I needed her to be for all of this to work. Or grab Lisandro's arm and tell him everything, that I was out of my depth here, that I had no better chance against The Coterie than our mother and father had.

But he didn't know any of that. He didn't even know I'd been up here before.

"You know what really kills me?" Hayden let out a bitter laugh. "You're walking around here like you're one of them, but you work for them. Maybe you wear nicer clothes than I do, maybe you stay in a nicer room than I do, but you work for them. They're paying you to be here. And yet you want to act like you're any other guest, like you have the right to make me pretend I'm happy to be in your presence."

"That's not what this is," I said. "I'm not what you think. I'm not like them."

"Oh yeah?" Hayden asked. "Then why am I standing here talking to you when I don't want to?"

Hayden kept going.

If I didn't slow her down, she was going to blow right past where she could see Lisandro. He'd be invisible to her even when he did appear.

But the rage in me went even deeper than that. I couldn't scream, so I wanted to tear down the stone of the garden walls. I wanted the sound of them crumbling to scream for me. My desperation streamed out of me, and it felt as solid as if I were growing branches. My fingers and my tongue were laurel leaves. I could feel the weight of the stone like it was in my hands.

I could feel everything crumbling.

"Stop!" The word broke from deep inside me.

As I yelled it, I could hear my voice blurring together with my brother's.

He saw it happening in the same moment I did. He saw it falling.

Hayden stopped.

A large stone tumbled away from the top of the garden wall.

It landed where Hayden would have been a second later if she hadn't heard us.

Hayden turned slowly, looking over her shoulder. As she did, she saw Lisandro in the distance, paled by the same evening mists I'd hidden in before.

Disbelief crossed her face. She'd heard how the ghost and I had spoken at the same time.

She looked between us with the same startled wonder, like I were an apparition as unbelievable as a ghost in the gardens.

With the fingers of my left hand, I lightly touched the hem of my right sleeve. Lisandro withdrew, appearing to vanish.

Hayden looked from where Lisandro had been, to the

fallen stone, to me. "You knew that was going to happen, didn't you?"

This should have been enough for me. Hayden now thought I communed with ghosts. She thought I had supernatural foresight.

But what she'd thought of me, who she'd thought I was, was a knife of frost against my anklebones. Her words still screamed inside me, and I still wanted to scream back.

"If that was anyone's loved one"—I looked toward where Lisandro had been—"I don't know it any more than you do."

Hayden was staring at me, not at the fallen rock, not at where Lisandro had appeared.

"I know the kinds of frauds you were talking about." I took a cautious step toward Hayden. "I know them because I was taken in by one after my mother and father died."

Shame pressed in on me from two sides like twin wraiths. One because of how I'd been fooled years ago. Another for how I was telling Hayden something true when I should have been telling every lie I could get away with.

"I wanted to talk to them so badly," I said. "I wanted to hear their voices again so badly that I was willing to pay anything I had. And I did."

Hayden's expression shifted. She believed me. That was the worst part, that Hayden seemed to believe me only when I said something true.

I had to keep any more of the truth from tumbling out of my mouth.

"That was how I figured out I had a real gift," I said, "by seeing frauds, exactly the kind you were talking about. I knew what I felt, what I could do, and I knew it was different from what they were doing."

That part was almost true.

"I can't contact anyone's lost loved ones," I said. "I can't get them messages from the other side."

That was all true.

"I can only communicate with whatever spirits are already here," I said.

There it was again, the stable ground of telling lies, solid under my feet.

And this time, Hayden believed. I could tell by her face that she believed.

LISANDRO

AS SOON AS Lola gave me the signal, I disappeared. But as I marked my path back toward the main building, my brain spun with everywhere I wanted Lola to avoid. Each garden wall. Every single flying buttress. Any and all doorway tops with ornamental friezes. Anything that could crash down onto her. From far away, The Coterie had looked like a glamorous fortress, but up close, it seemed held together with crafting paste.

I dodged under tree boughs, the branches hanging as low as streamers. But when I sensed someone on the other side of the branches, I froze. No one else was supposed to be out here. The guests were at dinner. The staff were either attending to them or having their own dinners.

I looked through the screen of the leaves, searching for the bright lilac of the dress my sister was wearing.

Instead, I saw the boy I'd seen earlier. I recognized his hands, his hair, the angle of his shoulders. He was sitting on the edge of a fountain. It was empty, running with neither water nor oil. Tendrils of vines were trying to pull it back into the earth, cracking the painted tiles.

The boy had his drawing paper again, this time with a few different pencils balanced on the edge of the book. As his arm moved in and out of the light, a scar flashed pale on his forearm. It was thin, sharp, and it connected a few clusters of freckles like the line mapping a constellation.

I shouldn't have been watching. But I wanted to know more about him. And I knew that this was all the more reason I shouldn't be watching.

Worse than watching, I was coming closer, slowly enough that I didn't make any more noise than the breeze through the branches.

The boy put down the pencil he was holding.

I stopped. I kept still.

But he didn't look my way. He shut his eyes, like he could feel the stirring in the air. His lips parted slightly, and a shiver went through his body that matched the one going through mine. He tilted his head, the light glancing over the side of his neck. It could have been nothing but him stretching. And yet the way he breathed in let me imagine my fingers were tracing that scar on his forearm. It let me imagine how his breathing might shift as I followed that constellation.

At the sound of footsteps, he and I both straightened up. I drew back far enough into the branches that whoever was approaching wouldn't see me.

Bixby Fairfax, a man I'd known only in newsprint, cut through the light. "Did you really think I wouldn't notice?"

The boy took up his sketching again, eyes on the paper. "Notice what?"

"Don't play stupid with me. You're stupid enough all on your own." He stood over the boy. "You're sending them money, aren't you?"

The boy's fingers tensed. His tendons cast thin shadows across the backs of his hands. "You know I'm not."

"If I knew that, do you think I'd be wasting my time talking to you instead of my guests?" Fairfax raised his hand.

I flinched, sure he was going to backhand the boy.

Papá had never raised a hand to me; how badly I'd wanted him to think me clever or brave or loyal steered me more than anyone's fists ever could have.

But when Fairfax raised his hand, I still flinched. I remembered every time I'd taken the back of a man's knuckles because he didn't like the look of me.

Fairfax knocked the sketchbook out of the boy's hands, sending the pencils flying everywhere.

The boy stared up at Fairfax. "You know I can't." His posture collapsed in, but he met Fairfax's eyes. "I couldn't send them anything even if I wanted to. You made sure of that."

"Not these stories of yours again," Fairfax said. "I thought Dr. Woodward straightened you out on all that."

"They're not stories," the boy said, the last word broken up by a cough.

"You may think you're here because Blythe is fond of you," Fairfax said. "But make no mistake. You're here because I let you stay."

The boy's shoulders trembled. It didn't look like fear, though. It was from the coughing he was holding at the back of his throat.

"I enjoy giving Blythe what she wants, even if it's hiring

some medium she read about in the newspaper," Fairfax said. "Even if it's having you around. But I have my limits."

As Fairfax left, he stepped on the pencils. One snapped under his polished shoe.

Once Fairfax was gone, the boy knelt on the ground, gathering up the pencils. He coughed harder, but not in the way I'd heard Lola at night the winter she was getting over pertussis. This sounded as though he was choking on something.

He cupped his hands under his mouth, gagging so hard I expected him to cough up blood or a tooth.

Then he pulled a damp cord from his mouth. His throat hitched as he drew it out. The whole length was covered in thin leaves like olive or eucalyptus. The horror of it was so contained, coiled into the small space between his hands and his mouth, and that somehow made it more awful, that someone might not notice if they weren't watching to begin with.

That rope of leaves, the wet gagging sounds he made, struck through the center of me, as though the cord were in my own throat. When they called Embry Fairfax possessed, was this what they meant?

His body relaxed, relieved to be breathing again. But it didn't show in his face. He stared at his hands in a way that seemed defeated. He blinked, and tears ran down his cheeks, not because he was crying but because his eyes had been watering. His wet eyelashes shone, catching the light as his breathing evened out.

Anyone who turned away at that moment might have felt sorry for him. Or maybe afraid of him. But a moment later,

Embry Fairfax lifted his head, glaring into the space where his father had been.

That wasn't the look of a worn-down boy.

That was the look of a prince capable of killing his father and taking his throne.

And for just that second, I wanted to watch him do it.

LOLA

IT WAS AS though the trees had wanted to help me. It was as though they knew how badly I'd wanted to stop Hayden, and they'd wound the fingers of their branches into a stone wall to help me do it.

But it had come at a price. I'd told more of the truth than I'd ever meant to. I'd let my rage be the brightest thing inside me. And I could feel the vines winding farther up my legs, clinging to my knees.

I was now a little less of a human girl and a little more of a girl becoming a tree.

A boy's yelling snapped me back to where I was. It was coming from the direction of the main building.

"You were there!" Embry was near a side door, yelling at Blythe. "You remember!"

His voice was more pleading than threatening.

Blythe's expression was one of mournful compassion.

"You know there's no use talking when you're like this,"

she said. "You're exhausted. A good night's sleep, that's the thing." She touched his arm.

He shrugged it off. "You know what he did!"

He was yelling loudly enough that faces were appearing in windows.

He was yelling loudly enough that within a minute, two men were on either side of him, herding him away from Blythe.

"You know I'm right!" Embry yelled over his shoulder at Blythe. "You know it."

As the men led him away, Blythe turned and saw me. She didn't look caught or embarrassed. She only gestured me into a side parlor. I thought she might call for tea, but instead she poured whiskey from a crystal decanter.

"I'm sorry you had to see that." She handed me a cut-crystal glass. "He gets himself very worked up. He's never been the same since his sisters abandoned the family."

The words were threads of gold in my hands. No one mentioned the Fairfax daughters except in whispers, and Blythe had just spoken of them at conversational volume. I'd barely arrived, and already she was trusting me with her confidences.

"Will he be all right?" I asked.

"Oh, yes." Blythe drained her glass, and even that she did delicately, artfully. "They just take him somewhere to rest. Everything around here can get agitating when you're overtired."

I tipped my own glass toward my mouth but didn't drink. It smelled like a rinse for a toothache.

Blythe poured herself another glass. "I hope this doesn't put you off us."

"We're all troubled in our own ways," I said. "Ghosts and those walking the earth."

"He's really a very nice boy," Blythe said. "Harmless, truly. Just given over to delusions sometimes."

"Blythe." I stopped her with a light smile.

Her face relaxed.

"You haven't scared me in the least." I raised my glass just enough for the crystal to catch the light. "And don't worry. Once I arrive, I never leave until a job's done."

LISANDRO

AS I MOVED behind the walls, voices echoed from the other side.

"Eugenia saw the ghost before the medium even arrived. Just last week, right out there in the gardens. A girl who looked positively stricken with sadness."

"Solomon swears he heard a woman's voice just a few nights ago."

Maybe Lola was right about us needing to act quickly. The suggestibility of the human mind was our best weapon, but if we waited, it could work against us. All it took was a couple of guests talking about an otherworldly girl or a pale, unfamiliar woman, then the rumor would spread, and that would be the ghost they'd expect.

We needed them talking about the unsettling apparition of a boy, the ghost of a young man with a frightening stare.

Lola hadn't been kidding about how shoddily this place had been built. The words came clear through the walls as I passed each guest room.

"It was a simple misunderstanding," a woman said. "It's nothing to write home about."

"Well, he didn't write home, did he?" a man said. "We had to learn about it in the papers. Court proceedings for unpaid tailor's bills? Is that the son we raised?"

"Can you blame him for seeing to his appearance?" the woman asked. "It was just a few suits."

"Don't you see that makes it all the worse?" the man asked. "That bill for two dozen pieces of custom clothing. He could have spent less on a carriage house full of cars."

I passed another room.

"A violet in the lapel," a woman was saying. "In June! Can you imagine?"

As I passed room after room, I heard laughter. Arguing. Gossiping. The low, kind murmurs of a husband getting his nauseated wife a cup of tea. Scraps of other people's lives.

Then a familiar pair of voices.

"Really, Bixby, more things?" Blythe asked. "We've talked about this. You can't buy everything you see on every trip."

"But some of these are presents for you," he said. "And presents for the house. Just let me show you." Fairfax sounded like an enthusiastic child, and Blythe like his hesitantly indulgent mother. "This dagger here, centuries old. Who do you know who has a better letter opener than that? And this as a paperweight, can't you see it? I've even bought a matching shield that would be perfect in the foyer."

"Have you ever considered that you might be a little too fond of acquiring things and not fond enough of simply having them?" Blythe asked. "If you keep going this way, we'll have no money and you'll have no space. No space, in your one-hundred-ninety-room estate."

And it was by listening to these conversations that I found out which of those one hundred and ninety rooms belonged to Fairfax's son.

"Do you think Fairfax will kick him out?" one woman asked. "Give his room to someone else?"

"The northeast corner of the top floor?" Another woman laughed. "Have you seen that room? Who would want it?"

Lola had told me about Embry Fairfax's reputation. Troubled. Dangerous. Possessed. And all that let me pretend I was doing this out of a sense of thoroughness. After all, anywhere we ran a job, we had to know all potential hazards.

Yes, there had been something dangerous in Embry Fairfax's eyes. But it didn't look like possession. It looked like he wanted vengeance for something, something even worse than his father bullying him. And I wanted to know what.

"Such an embarrassment," a man said. "Can you imagine your son having that kind of an outburst? And at the lady of the house no less?"

"I hear he's always been that way," another man said.

"Oh, that's not at all what I've heard," a woman said. "I was told he was a very agreeable child."

"Fairfax should send him off somewhere for good," the first man said. "Ship him off to wherever his sisters are hiding."

None of them spoke of a boy who grew leaves from his throat.

In a far corner of the top floor, I found a bedroom that seemed wedged into leftover space. Between the gaps where the oddly angled corners joined, I could look in from the other side of the wall.

The space had been decorated as opulently as any other suite—gold leaf on the ceiling, brocade drapes that fell from the tops of the windows and pooled on the floor, held aside by gold cords as thick as Lola's wrists. But iron staves, likely support for the decorative balconies, stuck out from the walls; you couldn't have turned out the lights without risking impaling yourself.

There was no closet or wardrobe. Embry Fairfax's clothing floated off the arms of the mounted candelabras, the jackets in clean shades of black and deep blue, the shirts gray and white. They looked more like the staff's uniforms, plain but carefully tailored. And yet he'd looked more rumpled than the members of the staff, as though he slept in his clothes.

The room was quiet, the bed made. The air seemed stale, and no dust motes swam in the light. There was no sign of Embry having been in here, and yet none of the chatter I'd heard spoke of where he was.

Then the sun highlighted a seam of gold on the opposite wall.

A mirror, hanging in a heavy faux-gilt frame, gave me an idea.

LISANDRO

"PLEASE TELL ME you have good news," Lola asked when I got back to our rooms. "Fairfax is breathing down my neck." She was combing her eyebrows in the mirror. "He stands right next to me during croquet; looks out over the guests with this creepy, wistful expression; and says, 'It gives me such satisfaction to entertain them,' like they're his children. Or like he'd created them himself or something."

Lola had talked this quickly, this relentlessly, the night before. It made it easy to simply not tell her what I'd seen with Embry. If I did, she'd want to know more. Her curiosity would propel her closer. She'd want to pick him apart the way she dismantled secondhand dresses. And I was caught between two different gravities. First, the pull of wanting to protect Lola from Embry Fairfax. Second, wanting to protect Embry Fairfax from Lola.

One made sense.

The other didn't.

Both conspired to keep me silent.

"And then he says, 'But it can be so tiresome to keep them entertained.'" Lola smoothed a curl of her wig. "Yes, I understand, you want everyone to see the ghost. Give me a minute. These people have no patience for how difficult a medium's work is."

"Speaking of which," I said, "I think I found a way we can do this."

That night, we wedged ourselves into the space between walls, gaps left either from the rushed construction or for planned insulation that had yet to be installed.

"You do realize that if we get caught, it might be a little difficult for my credibility to recover," Lola said.

"We won't get caught," I said. "The guests are all in Fairfax's private theater."

"Oh yeah," Lola said. "I heard everyone complaining about it earlier. It's always Blythe's films. Part of the price of admission of being a guest here, apparently. Mandatory cinematic merriment three nights a week at ten."

"What did you tell them?" I asked. "Did you feign a headache?"

"What kind of amateur do you think I am?" she asked. "A headache would've only gotten me out of tonight. I explained my spiritually sensitive constitution. Too much in the way of flashing lights could compromise my spectral intuitions."

"That almost sounds real."

"Doesn't it?" Lola was grinning when I looked back at her. "Blythe felt awful about it, thought I'd feel left out or something. But I assured her the quiet time would only benefit my process—allow me to wander the property seeking changes in the energetic currents." She tripped over a step.

I grabbed her arm to help her keep her balance. "Watch

out for those energetic currents, okay?" This back staircase, like so many in this building, was unfinished, the edges and walls still rough. The angles were something out of a science fiction movie.

"But what about the staff?" Lola asked. "There's a small army running this place. What are we going to do if they hear us?"

"They're all invited, too," I said. "And by invited, I mean practically required unless they claim an early bedtime for a morning shift."

"How do you know that?" she asked.

"I heard them talking," I said. "The guests aren't the only ones tired of it."

"Poor Hayden," Lola said. "Poor all of them. I hear it's the same films over and over. It's not even Blythe's complete canon. It's Fairfax's favorite selections. Meaning those horrible films he financed. The most awful versions of Juliet, Hedda Gabler, Cleopatra. All the roles that are least suited to her and that he talked her into because he wanted a dramatic actress on his arm, not a comedienne. I bet the only way the staff manages is by dozing off in the back rows."

A small unfinished window let in ambient light. It gleamed off the bread knife I had in my left hand and the crowbar gripped in my right.

"Are we planning to kill someone?" Lola asked.

"That would be an approach to haunting we've never tried before, but no, sorry to disappoint you." I knocked my fist into the plasterboard. "See this? It's cheap."

"I know it's cheap," she said. "I'm the one who told you how cheap."

"Well—" I shrugged and lifted the knife.

"You're going to cut into the house?" she asked. "Did you learn nothing from Mamá's bone-chilling version of 'Hansel and Gretel'?"

"No cellulose. No mineral wool. It's all so thinly constructed we can rip anything apart." I started sawing through the plasterboard. "All that money and he builds his dream palace out of straw."

"He wanted his dream palace in record time," Lola said. "That means he not only rushed the builders; he had to settle for whatever materials were available on short notice. The best craftsmen in the world couldn't have made a weathertight structure under those conditions."

I handed Lola the knife. "Hold this, okay?" I used the crowbar to pry away the plasterboard.

"What on earth are you doing?" she asked.

"It's a mirror." I scratched at a dark painted surface with the end of the crowbar. "And a really shitty one, like every other mirror in this place except for a few antique ones in the foyer and the dining room."

"What's the point of that?" Lola asked.

"Think about it." I kept scratching at the paint. "You can't invite rich and famous guests without catering to their vanity with wall-size looking glasses."

"And when you burn through your entire construction budget on antiques and rush jobs, you don't have money left for a good mirror, much less a hundred of them," Lola said. "I get it. But why are you—" Then it came to her. The basic materials science, the kind we used for our acts all the time.

I was scratching through the silvering aluminum and the dark paint backing on a cheap mirror. It was preparation for an optics-fueled magic trick.

"You're making one-way glass," she said.

"Exactly. And now"—I had scratched a hole in the coating large enough that she could stick her face in it like a window, seeing into the guest room—"I can materialize inside a mirror. I'll pull the plasterboard panel aside when I want to appear and put it back when I want to vanish. If I do it slowly enough, it'll look like the whole scene is simply disappearing."

"And with the plasterboard back behind the glass," she said, "it'll look like a regular mirror again."

"Exactly," I said. "We stop the rumors about the ghost girl before they get any more traction."

Lola straightened up from examining the mirror. "The rumors about what?"

"You know how this works," I said. "Everyone's on edge here, so they start seeing things."

"Like what?" Lola sounded irritated. I didn't like that note in her voice. It was a little too much like the one she'd had when she'd seen the Magnificent Karina.

I breathed out, praying that Lola would take this as the small, manageable hitch it was. Ever since we'd gotten here, Lola hadn't quite been the sister I knew. The sister I knew almost relished the challenges a job threw at us. She almost seemed to think of them as a game. But this Lola was getting thrown off her balance by every pebble in the road. To this Lola, a skeptical bartender had been reason to throw out our plans. To this Lola, an impatient millionaire was reason to rush.

"A couple of guests were talking about some ghostly girl they saw last week," I said. "It's nothing. At least it'll be nothing once we get started."

In the low light, I couldn't quite parse the expression on

my sister's face. She almost seemed angry. "Did they say what she looked like?"

"She didn't look like anything," I said. "Because she's not real. And by the time we're done, no one's going to talk about any ghost except the one we want them talking about. Now help me with this, okay?"

By the end of that night, we had three mirrors ready.

By the next morning, I had appeared in all of them, just for a few seconds, as fast and elusive as a trick of the light.

"Nicely done." Lola toasted me with her teacup over breakfast. "I went out for an early stroll, and the whispers are already starting." She folded over the society pages. When they wouldn't bend neatly, she tossed them at me the way she always did. "I can just smell the gossip." She breathed in like she was inhaling the scent of climbing roses in the air.

She seemed calmer this morning, settled now that we knew our next steps.

"Speaking of gossip." I smoothed out the pages she'd crumpled. "You haven't seen Fairfax's son around, have you?"

Lola regarded me, amused. "Look at you, wanting to know everyone's business. I knew I'd be a good influence on you eventually. And no, not since his little monologue I told you about."

"You don't think it's strange?" I asked. "He's here and then suddenly he's not?"

"Maybe Fairfax sent him to his mother's," Lola said. "Maybe Fairfax banished him for the cardinal sin of making a scene at a party. Maybe he ran off and is keeping company with coyotes. What do you care?"

"But what was he making a scene about?" I asked.

"How would I know?"

"That's exactly it." I folded the newsprint along its creases. "You're usually the one who wants to know everything in the universe that everyone else is talking about. Why don't you care?"

"Because he's a Fairfax," Lola said. "And that means anything out of his mouth is a lie."

"You don't know that," I said.

"Don't I?" Lola asked. "Fairfax has cooked books on a dozen businesses. Not even cooked. Broiled. Flambéed. He's faked profits. He's structured companies in ways just this side of pyramid schemes."

"But he and his father aren't the same person," I said. "I don't get it. You're the one who always wants to know every possible piece of information. You want to know what kind of wood framing is holding up a house you're haunting."

"Because it informs my character," she said. "Cedar attracts ghosts of a very different temperament than walnut."

"And yet you don't want to know more here?" I asked.

"No," she said. "Because I know everything I need to know. And trust me"—she snatched the folded newsprint from my hand—"so do you."

LOLA

THAT NIGHT, I dreamed of branches sucking the blood and the life out of me. I dreamed of them stabbing their splintery fingers into my back and drawing out my heart. The next morning, the knobs of my spine looked like knots of wood. They formed a thin, textured trunk running down the middle of my back. There was no blood, no broken skin. How cleanly they'd emerged only turned my stomach more, as though this had been inside me all along, as though I had always been a girl destined to transform into something else.

It wasn't just vines on my legs now. The center of me was turning.

I steadied my hands and put on the most modest of the Magnificent Karina's dresses. I set my mouth into the smile I'd need whenever a curious guest tried to engage me in conversation.

"Are you all right?" Lisandro asked. "Your face looks like you're posing for a hair tonic ad."

"Never better," I said, and I was gone before he could ask any more questions.

While the guests were out lawn bowling or on drives around the property—and the members of the staff had the unenviable task of waiting for their requests—I went to work on the salon.

In the past twenty-four hours, Lisandro had become a sensation at The Coterie. Those who had seen him told the story over and over—*It was only a moment, yet it seemed as though he stopped time, as though he was before me for hours.* Some who hadn't seen him pretended they had—*Yes, he was right outside my window, floating.*

Some swore they'd heard him, as though he was summoning the living from the other side—*He was calling to me, clear as church bells. It gave me such a chill. A voice like a windstorm. I've never heard anything like it.*

The more walls we prepared, the more appearances my brother could make. He could drift like a shadow from room to room, keeping guests wondering where they might spot him next. So I cleared away the wall and enough of the backing on a mirror that I could see into the salon, imagining which sofas and settees would get the best view of the ghost.

The salon was empty, but the door from the salon into the hall framed none other than Embry Fairfax. Or a rough approximation of him. His posture was loose, like his body was a suit draped on the hanger of his shoulders.

Blythe stepped into the frame, as neat and tidy as Embry was unkempt. His shirt was rumpled, his hair mussed. But compared with when I'd last seen him, he looked unnervingly tranquil, like they'd given him laudanum.

"Are you feeling any better?" Blythe straightened his necktie like a mother.

"Much." Embry's voice was flat but crisp. No slurring. "Thank you for asking."

Then they were both gone from the frame.

Soon my porthole gave me a clear view of the rest of the salon. Fairfax's favorite chair. Blythe's favorite lamp. The bar where Hayden stirred up the guests' drinks.

The bar was clear now, except for that well-worn copy of *Metamorphoses*.

I'd told Hayden far too much. I needed to prove myself better at divining secrets than telling them. And getting a look at any notes Hayden had written was a start. You could learn a lot from someone by how they talked back to their books.

I wound my way out from behind the walls; made sure my dress, wig, and eyelashes looked presentable; and sneaked into the empty salon.

A quick turn through the pages didn't show any notes. But there was a notch in the threaded band of the book's spine, and not just because a ribbon was marking the place. This part was clearly a favorite. Hayden had turned to it enough times to change the shape of the book itself.

I opened to where the ribbon was, careful not to tear the delicate pages.

"What are you doing?"

I slammed the book shut.

Hayden stood in the doorway, holding a brass tray.

She was wearing trousers today. Secondhand ones, judging from the wear on the edges of the hem and waistband. But elegant ones, like a fashionable socialite might wear on horseback. Her hair was tucked behind her ears, the ends brushing her neck.

I set the book down on the bar. "You know when someone you know is reading a book you really like and you want to know what part they're on?"

"You know *Metamorphoses*." Hayden started loading highball glasses onto the tray. "Something changes into something else. You've read one part, you've read them all."

Maybe Hayden no longer thought I was a fraud, but she was so guarded I couldn't find my way in. I hadn't gotten the good look I'd wanted at the book, either. But I'd caught the name of a single character. Iphis. And when I got back to my room, I took out the copy that had belonged to Papá. It had become so well-worn over the years that I'd had to sew it back together more than once.

When I found the story about Iphis, I skimmed the pages, trying to remember it. It wasn't one I came back to over and over, and it wasn't one I remembered Papá reading to us, so it hadn't worn a path in my brain. But as I read now, I had an idea.

"I know how we're getting the dry ice," I said.

"How?" Lisandro asked from his room.

"Hayden." I sat up on my bed. "The baby bartender. When I'm done, she'll do anything I want."

"Impressive," Lisandro said. "But again I ask, how?"

Why did Lisandro always sound wary whenever I had my best ideas?

"Hayden's lovesick," I said.

"How do you know that?" he asked.

"Because I know." I lifted the book, pointing at the story of

Iphis and the heartless princess who not only refused his love but also mocked him with such ruthlessness that Aphrodite turned her to stone. "And here's the saddest part. If this is the story she keeps coming back to, she's probably lovesick for someone she thinks is out of her reach. Maybe even a guest here. So I'm going to help unite her with the object of her love."

"And there it is." Lisandro pointed at the air between us.

"What?" I asked.

"The bad idea. I knew it was coming."

"And why exactly is this a bad idea?" I asked.

"You came, you saw, you convinced a skeptic that you're the genuine article," he said. "What more do you want?"

"It's not enough," I said.

"Why not?" Lisandro asked.

"Because I made a mistake." The words came tumbling out of my mouth. "And now she thinks we're equals instead of me being on the supernatural pedestal I need to be on to pull this off."

Lisandro blinked at me. "What are you talking about?"

"I told Hayden how we got started with this." I flopped back onto the bed. "Well, how I got started."

"Why would you do that?"

"Because I couldn't stand her thinking that we take money from grieving families." I stared up at the wallpapered ceiling, patterned with swans or geese or some other long-necked waterfowl wearing golden crowns. "Because I couldn't stand her thinking that we were like that woman."

There was a shift in weight. Lisandro was now sitting on my bed near me. Even without looking at him, I could tell by his posture he was a lot calmer than my confession deserved.

"You must not have told all of it," he said.

"No, of course not," I said. "I just told her that it was how I realized I had otherworldly gifts, because encountering frauds helped me understand the difference between what they were doing and what I could do."

"So what's the problem?" Lisandro asked. "You had real feelings, and you thought quickly enough to do something with them. It's what you do."

How nice he was being made me feel worse about everything he didn't know.

The lies I'd told him.

The money I'd taken and then put back before he could notice.

That I was becoming half girl, half tree.

"You plan as best you can, and if the plan goes wrong, you improvise," Lisandro said. "Remember the time you convinced that shipping magnate you were the angel of ice storms?" A laugh came into his voice. "The angel of ice storms. In California."

With every understanding word from my brother, my guilt curdled into shame.

"So what if it wasn't the original plan?" he asked. "So what if you told Hayden a little more than you wanted to? You pulled it off. It worked."

"This coming from you?" I asked. "You, who'd have time stamps on our performances down to the second if you could? Have you been breathing fumes in the crawl spaces? We can't have people knowing anything about who we actually are. Once upon a time, you would have been the one telling me that."

Light, tapping footsteps came from the hallway. A series of staccato knocks landed on the door.

I sat up. Lisandro stood up.

"Pardon the intrusion," Blythe sang from the other side of the door.

"Hide," I whispered to Lisandro.

"Way ahead of you." As quiet as a cat, he disappeared into his room.

I answered the door with a placid smile.

"I do hate to disturb you." Blythe was wearing a different outfit than she had been this morning. A tangerine suit, the sleeves and skirt cut perfectly to her proportions. "But I just couldn't help myself." Her smile was bright, but the muscles around her eyes were tense. "The guests are saying they're hearing the ghost of a boy, seeing him, even."

I nodded, appropriately thoughtful.

"Bixby's pleased." She was forcing her smile now. "The guests are thrilled at the excitement. I feel as though no one takes this seriously but me. Won't the ghost be offended at us all making light of his torment?"

I tilted my head to the side, as though considering very hard.

Just as Blythe looked about to say something, I put my hands on the sides of her face. I had to stop her before she got any bright ideas about inviting herself in.

I stared into the crystal blue of her eyes.

"You are the gentlest of souls, aren't you?" I said.

Her lips parted in a wondering expression.

"I feel the boy's presence very strongly. Sometimes as though he's even in the room with me." After a long, meaningful pause, I dropped my hands from her cheeks. "There's no need to worry. All will be well in good time."

"I'm so relieved to hear you say that." Her breath out was

almost a laugh. "Because the ladies convinced Bixby to throw another one, and I was feeling so conflicted over it. I thought maybe such an exuberant celebration might be inappropriate."

"Convinced him to throw another what?" I asked.

She handed me a square of stiff, heavy stationery. "You are cordially invited to your first Coterie costume ball."

"Oh," I said. "I didn't bring any costumes"—except the ones that turned me into the Magnificent Karina—"but I'm sure I'll come up with something."

"No need." Blythe's party-girl shimmer had returned. "I brought just the thing."

I hadn't noticed the large golden box on the floor until she reached for it now.

"It's one of my costumes from last season." She thrust it into my hands. "It was a mistake. The color didn't suit me. But it'll be ravishing on you, especially with your hair. You'll be the green fairy. I can't wait."

She trotted off.

I took the box inside, set it on the low sitting room table, and drew out the dress. It was as bright green as absinthe, with ribbons of darker green fabric flowing down the front like kelp.

"What on earth is that?" Lisandro asked.

I turned it and got the full picture of the draping. "My costume, apparently."

The gown was practically backless. It would show what I was hiding not only from everyone at The Coterie but from my own brother.

"Do we have any spare wire hangers?" I rummaged through the Magnificent Karina's dresses.

Lisandro went back toward his room.

I gripped two sides of a light yellow dress and looked heavenward. "God forgive me for destroying such a beautiful piece of your creation." I ripped the chiffon from the neckline to the skirt hem.

The tearing sound pulled Lisandro back. "What are you doing?"

"Improvising." I took the hangers from him. "If they want a green fairy, I'll give them a green fairy."

"She gave you a costume," Lisandro said. "I really don't think you need to work that hard."

"Well, one of us has to," I said.

Lisandro blinked. "Excuse me?"

I was being awful, and I knew it. But I felt my brother's logic, his perceptive gaze, closing in on me, and all I wanted was to shove it away.

"Maybe you could spend a little more time working on your character and a little less time worrying about sad little rich boys," I said.

"What is that supposed to mean?" he asked.

"You think I don't know why you feel sorry for him?" I asked. "Not every gay boy in the world deserves your sympathy, you know."

The shift in my brother's expression was so slight, a flattening of the line of his mouth, a change at the edges of his eyes. But I knew him well enough to know I'd crushed him.

"Lis—" I said.

He held up a hand, not looking at me. "Don't."

That gesture plus that one word, that signature Lisandro Bernal combination, warned me not to say anything else.

LOLA

I HATED EVERYTHING. I hated the dusk tinting the stone arches purple. I hated the Victrola with its cloyingly festive music and its horn like a giant nightmare morning glory. I hated my green dress and my yellow wings and what an awful sister I was. I hated this stupid costume ball, where I had to be instead of trying to get my brother to talk to me.

I passed women dressed as princesses or as mermaids with gowns so thickly sequined they looked as though they had scales. There was a quartet of actresses coordinating as the queens in a playing card deck, each a different suit. The men dressed as jesters or jousting knights, or they wore their finest dinner jackets but with donkey ears or an oversize top hat worthy of the Mad Hatter.

Every gaudy detail was a gnat buzzing around me.

I wove through the crowd with a smile, making sure the chiffon-covered wire of my wings didn't hit anyone in the face or knock a tray of drinks out of a waiter's hands. I smiled even as I wanted to punch in every jester's hat and papier-mâché costume head. There was gossip everywhere, and I kept waiting for it to lift my sour mood. I overheard whispers about affairs. "And when she found out, she threw a crystal dish full of candied chestnuts straight at his head. Not because he had a mistress. But because his mistress was too plain, in her opinion. Insultingly so."

Tales of a debutante ball: "You should have seen the fighting. Otherwise well-bred young ladies tearing each other's hair out over which signature scent belonged to whom. Gwin laid her claim to verbena with the ferocity of a mother bear, and Francine was willing to fight to the death over Parma violet."

Details about a guest set to arrive next week: "I heard she tried to get out of paying the tariffs by hiding her new jewels and her rolls of silk and lace in a bustle. What could have gotten into her? Our mothers hardly wore bustles. Did she really think a customs officer wouldn't raise an eyebrow?"

And among the young men, complaints about the inadequate flow of money from their trust funds:

"My mother doesn't understand the bills. What does she expect? What self-respecting gentleman wears anything other than silk for his undergarments?"

"I had to discard all my suits when the changes came to the hems. It would've been uncivilized not to."

"My father fails to realize that thirty pairs of shoes a year *is* economizing."

Then, in those tangles of gossip, I found another thread, one so bright with energy it sounded illuminated. I felt the electricity of it even before I understood the words.

"I could barely believe my eyes."

"He looked so very mournful."

"I could sense something in the air just before he appeared."

Chatter about the ghost was bubbling through the party. It was everywhere.

And so were the jealous, pinched expressions of those who hadn't seen him themselves.

The Coterie was already the most exclusive resort there was. I'd overheard starlets on the telephones whispering, *You wouldn't truly understand unless you saw it yourself* in a way designed to make their friends envious. The *Wish you were here* postcards of the castle-like facade rubbed it in. Only the most privileged were guests here.

Now my brother's appearances created a new divide. Now there were the privileged among the most privileged. And that was enough to drive everyone else to distraction.

"I bet she didn't really see him," I heard one socialite say to another. "She'd do anything to stand out. And with such ordinary cheekbones, can you blame her?"

Apparitions of my brother were becoming the most coveted accessory here. He was handsome enough to thrill the young ladies and threaten the men who wanted their attention. His eyes, as dark as the night sky over the hills, added to the sense that he was an old photo come to life, a living daguerreotype. I'd perfected his costume, adding pin tucks and gathered sleeves to his too-big shirt so that he looked like a lovesick wanderer, a shipwrecked sailor, a lost poet from ages past. He was fodder for whatever story the guests wanted to give him. We lit him from underneath with green light, so that he seemed to emit an ethereal glow. And thanks to our rehearsals, his expression was at once stricken, sad, and tinged with foreboding, as though he carried some frightening prophecy. My brother was memorable enough to obliterate any recollections of me haunting The Coterie as a ghostly girl.

This was going better than we could have dreamed, and I kept waiting for the thrill of it to land. But it was dampened and flat, because I was the worst sister in the world. My brother didn't want to hear anything from me right now, not even this.

As I passed the bar, Hayden slid a low glass toward me.

"You look like you could use a drink," she said.

It was purple, garnished with a deep-blue pansy.

"You may be a real medium"—Hayden leaned over the bar enough to lower her voice—"but you're younger than I am."

"What's that got to do with the price of eggs?" I asked, my eyes meeting hers. I needed to show her that nothing she knew about me, nothing she could guess, could rattle me. "And how's it any of your business?"

"I'm not judging." Hayden lowered her voice further but didn't whisper. With the chatter glittering around the costume ball, she didn't need to. "I lied about my age, too. But if you want to fit in around here, if you don't want them to treat you like a little girl they can push around, they need to think you can drink with them. And if you want to keep up with the socialites, you need a signature aperitif. This one's called an Aviation."

"I appreciate the gesture," I said. "But I don't drink."

"And I'm not serving you." Hayden wiped down an ice bucket. "That's the teetotaler's version. Grenadine. Imitation crème de violette. No alcohol. But it's the same color as the real thing. They'll never know."

I took a cautious sip.

She was telling the truth. There was no bite of alcohol. Only sugar.

"Is this your version of an apology?" I asked.

She cut a grapefruit in half, knife right through the middle. "You know, I thought of making you a zero-proof version of another cocktail. Pale green. Touch of maraschino. Lime. But I couldn't figure out how to duplicate the Chartreuse. Too bad, too, because that's the one that really would have suited you."

"Why's that?" I asked.

"Because it's called the Last Word"—she glanced up at me—"and you seem like a girl who really likes getting it."

This drink, and the slight smile at the corner of Hayden's mouth, was as much of an opening as I'd get.

"You might like my last word," I said.

"Oh yeah?" Hayden seemed amused as she poured amber liquid over sprigs of lavender. "Why's that?"

I took a candied cherry from one of the little bowls on the bar. "Because I'm going to help you."

"I appreciate the sentiment," Hayden said, "but I work alone."

"I don't mean with the drinks." I leaned over the bar. "I'm going to help you win your true love's heart."

"My what?" Hayden asked.

"The object of your affections." I looked around but kept my voice low. "So who is it? Is it someone here? You can tell me. I promise I won't tell a soul. Living or dead."

"The object of my affections?" Hayden asked. "When did I get one of those?"

"Don't worry," I said. "It's obvious to me, but I have a gift for these things. I promise you it's not obvious to anyone else."

Now Hayden looked both amused and as though she was

humoring me. "This should be good. Is this when you tell me that if I clip my fingernails at three in the morning during a gibbous moon that I'll find true love?"

"But you already have. And I understand your need for discretion, so let me put it in a way that only a reader of Ovid would understand." I leaned in so close my toes were barely touching the ground now. "Is it safe to say you have a certain kinship with the story of Iphis?"

Hayden's rhythm of quick, efficient motions paused.

"Iphis," I whispered. "The lovesick shepherd."

All traces of Hayden's amusement evaporated.

"I'm going to ask this nicely once. I will ask more than once if I have to, but, I promise you, it'll be far less polite the second time." She turned a twist of lemon over a lit match. "What you're doing here, please leave me out of it."

"I'm just trying to help," I said.

"If you want to help, then stop." Hayden plunged the blackened match into water. "Just stop."

She looked at me with such forbidding intensity that my feet sank back down to the ground. The vines on my legs felt as though they were pulling me into the earth.

"I thought you wanted to be friends," Hayden said. "Not pry me open to see what you could guess about me. These people might have hired you to come dig around in their lives, but I didn't."

Growing applause turned my head.

Blythe was making her entrance. She wore a long-sleeved gown with a base of sheer fabric that would have revealed everything if it hadn't been covered with leaves. Hundreds of them, some embroidered, some made of fabric, some embellished with jewels like drops of rain. They looked sealed to her skin as though she were growing them from her body. A tiara of crystal-adorned fabric leaves added to the illusion that she was half woman, half tree.

Fairfax came forward, clad in something Henry VIII might have worn for a royal portrait. "My forest queen." He bowed deeply, kissing Blythe's hand.

"I'm a dryad," she said, laughing softly. "I told you that."

Dryad.

The word seared into me.

My rage toward this place was turning me from a girl into a tree. But to Blythe, those leaves were nothing but a costume. To Blythe, anything could be cut up and stitched back together into a costume. Anything could be rearranged to look like a party. Her only care in the world was the ghost drifting through her walls, and even that was a problem she thought she could pay to solve.

My bones shifted like branches. The prickling under my skin felt like leaves trying to break through to the light.

I could feel my anger flashing through the boughs above me, so brightly I could almost see it, like lighting illuminating the wood. The trees above me twisted and groaned in the night breeze. They made noise like the creaking of floorboards during a windstorm.

I didn't pinpoint the sound until I saw the stone arch crumbling above where Blythe stood.

For a fraction of a second, I considered doing nothing. I considered letting the stone fall and crush her. But if I did, I couldn't face my mother's and father's memories. I couldn't face my own brother.

I shoved Blythe out of the way, so artlessly that a distant observer would have thought I was starting a catfight.

Then the keystone fell from the middle of the arch. The ones next to it crumbled. As they crashed down, the guests skittered back.

The pile of stone settled where the two of us had been seconds earlier. Where the center of the arch had loomed in the air, thin laurel branches now dangled loose like frayed wires.

"It's all right!" Fairfax stretched out his arms, distorting the enormous sleeves of his costume. "Just a little earthquake." He peppered his words with a laugh.

With that laugh, the alarm on Blythe's face turned to horror. Her friends and maids were gathering in, fussing over her, offering glasses of water and cups of wine, offering to escort her somewhere to lie down. But whatever string held Blythe together—a hat ribbon, a silver thread, a length of celluloid film—snapped.

She grabbed my hand. Hard. She pulled me through the gardens, toward the house, through an ornately carved side door I'd never been through.

She knew.

Blythe knew who I was. Why I was here. Maybe even what I was hiding under my wire-and-chiffon wings.

Blythe led me through a hallway paved with white marble, punctuated with columns like the ones surrounding the pool. At the end of it was a pair of doors, flanked with a pair of fountains, each a wide golden bowl that streamed into a marble basin.

She pushed through the double doors, and we were in a vast shimmering room. Tiny squares of clear glass covered the walls and ceiling. Tiny squares of cobalt paved a deep pool. This must have taken years. It was a task straight out of a myth.

The golden ceiling seemed as distant as the sky. The tiled pool looked endlessly deep, an ocean within four walls.

Easily deep enough for Blythe to drown me.

I could twist out of her hold. I could win a fight against her. My fingernails could scratch up that pretty face.

Then she dropped my hand.

"This is a disaster." Blythe was balling her fists against her chest, rumpling the leaves on her dress. "This is all a disaster."

She hadn't brought me here to drown me.

She was frantic.

"Look!" She jabbed a finger. "Look at that!"

Tiles were crumbling off the walls. At first, I hadn't noticed, but now I couldn't miss the scattered spaces left bare, showing the mortar underneath. In the seconds we stood there, another golden square dropped into the dark blue water.

"He pretends not to see it," Blythe said. "This place is falling apart, and he doesn't want to see it. He doesn't even return the accountant's calls when he tells him what it takes to heat all these rooms in winter. All he does is continue to buy things while the walls are crumbling. And he wants everyone to think it's just earthquakes!"

The panicked way she looked everywhere at once, how she was nearly rubbing the varnish off her nails, shifted something in me. It left the bitter twist of something unfamiliar on my tongue. I had painted my own expression with compassion so well that I was almost beginning to feel it.

"It's been happening for years," she said. "Even when we were still building. But it's gotten so much worse lately."

The official story about Blythe Bell was that she'd come from a family who ran a midsize, very prosperous lace factory.

But looking at her now, seeing her fear, I doubted it. A girl who came from money wouldn't have been so quick to attach herself to such a foolish man. Young ladies with money married men who seemed respectable at first glance, whose destructive eccentricities didn't become obvious until after the wedding. But Bixby Fairfax was such a blatant risk that only a woman desperate for money, desperate to keep the lack of it in her past, would have taken the gamble.

Myths were full of women who'd been taken in by men's deceptions. A ruthless god could seduce a woman by making himself seem like a hundred beautiful things. A swan. A white bull. A bright flame. A shower of gold. What had Fairfax promised Blythe? What had he made himself look like?

"Why do you do it?" I asked.

Her eyes paused on me. "Do what?"

"Everything he wants you to do," I said. "Your last pictures, they've all been roles he's wanted you in."

I didn't have to say the rest. The critics had said it all. Blythe Bell was a born comedic actress, an ingenue who'd transitioned seamlessly into screwball romps. She could pinwheel her eyes as though seeing stars. She could faint in an overdone way that left audiences roaring with laughter.

That was before Fairfax. He wanted her to be a proper actress, and to him, that meant a dramatic actress. He kept buying her way into roles like Anne Boleyn, Ophelia, Lady Guinevere. The results had been so horrible that Lisandro and I stopped spending our dimes to see them.

Blythe's face registered no offense. Her persona was coming back, the sweet shrugging, the liveliness in the eyes. She was raising her gleaming shields again.

"Everyone has a bad run now and then," she said.

"But it's not even your bad run," I said. "It's his."

"And what kind of wife would I be if I held a little bad luck against him?"

Except she wasn't a wife. Fairfax wouldn't even marry her. He still insisted that openly having a mistress was more respectable than divorce.

He had managed to keep a different woman under each of his thumbs.

"What are you going to do when he runs through his grandfather's money?" I asked.

"That won't happen," she said.

"It could, and you know it. I think you know it better than he does."

This was when Lisandro would have told me to stop talking. My mouth was running ahead of me.

This was usually the feeling that got me into a screaming match or a fight in a bar, not trying to talk reason into a starlet twice my age. She was like some ancient princess. I could see her sealing her own fate with every step toward that swan, that flame, that shower of gold.

"The jewels he gives you," I said. "One day you're going to be selling them so he can shore up a hastily built mansion. Or so he can keep buying things that will stay crated up because he doesn't have the room for them."

"No." She gave a laugh as light as puff pastry. "Men like him, they don't fail. Not for good. They always pick themselves up. They always find a way."

Whatever compassion I had now shuttered closed. Not because she was as foolish as Bixby Fairfax, but because she was right. Men like him didn't fail. They simply found other doors being held open by white-gloved attendants.

"Yes," I said, "but would such men ever succeed without the counsel of a wise woman at their side?"

Her bright shield lowered just a little. She looked flattered. Curious.

"You take seriously what he ignores," I said. "The crumbling of his country house while a haunting rages within the walls, and he considers them unrelated. A mere coincidence."

"You think the ghost is doing this?" she asked. "Everything falling apart, you think it's because of the haunting?"

There it was. Gold threads dropped into my hands. All I had to do was take them and weave something wondrous.

"It would explain the chill," I said. "Why it's so difficult to heat the rooms even in a warm season. Spirits can have that effect on the air."

I turned my face to the tiled ceiling, considering for an unnecessarily long time. I made Blythe wait so long that she fidgeted with the crystal beading on the leaves of her dress.

"There's so much, isn't there?" I said.

"What do you mean?" she asked.

"You sense so much more than those around you, don't you?" I took her face in my hands, one thumb under each of her sparkling blue eyes. "It's your greatest and most precious gift. Even more than your beauty. Even more than the talents that made you a star."

Deception is a prestigious art form. It takes an artist to tell someone exactly what they want to hear.

"But it also means that so much more troubles you than troubles everyone else," I said. "Doesn't it?"

I stared at her long enough that tears gathered in the corners of her eyes, reflecting all the gold and deep blue around us.

"Everything I've done," she said, her voice threadbare,

"it's all been to protect Bixby, to protect what he's built. Everything. And it's all falling apart."

Maybe she'd been lured by Fairfax just as ancient princesses had been lured by white bulls. But she'd made her choice.

So had I. She may have been an ancient princess, but I was Circe snapping my fingers. I was Aphrodite smiling as hounds tore apart my enemies. I was the dragon who could cast scales onto the bodies of anyone who tried to slay me.

"Then we'll have to put it all back together," I said in my most reassuring whisper. "Isn't that what we women always do?"

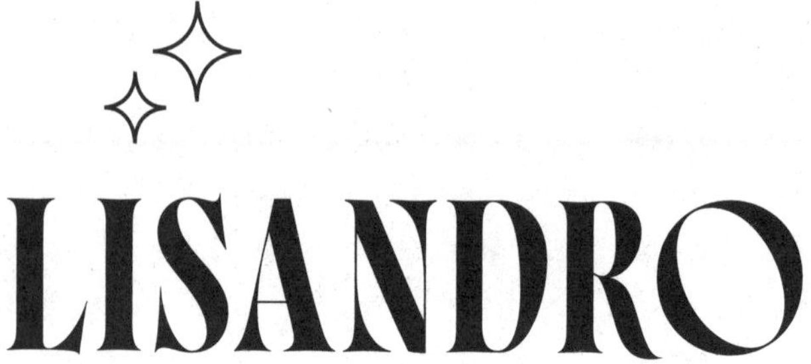

LISANDRO

I COULD BARELY look at my sister.

But that didn't stop me from admiring how artfully we were haunting The Coterie.

We'd positioned lanterns to illuminate me from underneath. We'd put fabric under the bottom edge of each plasterboard panel so there'd be no noise as I slid it to the side. We'd even managed a rough map of these hundred and ninety rooms.

This was our way, on every job. Setup. Strategy. Performance. Collect our fees. Do everything as cleanly and with as little risk as possible.

So I knew better than to go near Embry Fairfax, the boy everyone said was dangerous, the boy who vanished and reappeared at The Coterie as though he, too, were a ghost.

It would just be this once. I wouldn't even let him see me.

When I got to the space behind his mirror, odd noises came through from the other side. It was a syncopated thudding and knocking around, like someone was moving furniture.

I slid the panel a little out of place, enough that I could see into the room, but not enough that anyone could see me.

One of the guests, older than I was but young in comparison with most of the men, was tearing the room apart. The fabric and pattern of his suit marked him as a guest, not a member of the staff. He was emptying trunks, overturning drawers, scattering papers.

Just as he was ripping apart the bedcovers, Embry Fairfax appeared at the door.

Embry's eyes darted, following the wafting papers. "What are you doing?"

"Your father asked me to do a little inspection of your room." When the man grinned, his teeth gleamed as brightly as the jeweled bar on his tie. "Make sure you weren't hiding anything."

Embry gathered up papers. "Like what?"

"Anything." The man stood over him. His hair was as dark as his skin was pale, and the bright green of his eyes must have gotten him anything his money couldn't. "Items that have gone missing. Obscene literature."

Embry had his back to the man. But I could see the shame rounding his shoulders.

The man picked up a tiny glass jar filled with leaves. "What's this?"

Embry whirled around. "Put that down."

"Specimen collection?" The man held it away as Embry grabbed for it. "Is that why they call girls like you evening botanists?"

The hitch of shame deepened in Embry. He was someone who seemed to grow ashen rather than red when embarrassed.

Evening botanist. I'd been called that before. I would've

known what it meant even if the man hadn't called Embry a girl.

Going near Embry Fairfax was beyond foolish. Going near any boy I felt anything for was beyond foolish, especially during a job. It was like deciding to swim near a whirlpool because you liked the glassy shine of the swirling water. That was how you got pulled under. You lost the ability to tell the difference between what was merely beautiful and what was strong enough to destroy you.

I turned on the lantern.

I slid the panel aside.

"I see the hand of death on your shoulder," I said.

When the man looked my way, my accusing stare was waiting for him.

"Yes," I said breathlessly, making my voice waver. "The clutching hand of death."

The glass jar fell from the man's fingers and thudded to the carpet.

"It crawls toward your throat." I curled a hand near my face, imitating Lola's gestures of horror. "It wraps its cold fingers about your neck."

The man bolted from the room.

"It follows you now!" I called after him, in my best version of how Lola would call out, as if warning someone from the other side.

Embry turned, slowly, toward the mirror.

His eyes were as wide as the man's had been. The difference was he didn't seem afraid. He looked at me as though I was something so wondrous I could inspire awe. A comet. A moonbow. A sheet of lighting illuminating the entire sky.

"Thank you." He sounded touched, the way he might have been surprised by any kind gesture.

I knew, instantly, the magnitude of my mistake. I was meant to be a brief apparition. Instead, I'd intervened.

If I hadn't already understood the depth of my error, I would have the moment Embry smiled at me and said, "I knew it."

LOLA

BLYTHE RETURNED TO the costume ball with her best face on. She raised her glass—"To defying death!" She lured guests into dancing. She took her most glittering form.

The younger men danced among the fallen rocks as though daring fate. Even Fairfax was in a good enough mood to toast in my direction—"To the heroine of the hour!"

As the evening wore on, talk about Lisandro peppered all conversation.

"I hear he looks young."

"I hear he looks ageless."

"You mean like a vampire?"

The fallen archway only added to the intrigue.

"Do you think the ghost was angry?"

"Do you think he meant the rocks to fall on someone?"

"He couldn't have meant them to fall on Blythe. Who would have anything against her?"

"But who was standing near her? Does anyone remember?"

"Do you think if we asked the ghost very nicely, he might

tumble some down onto Thurston's head? Knock some sense into him?"

"Why don't we ask the medium what she thinks happened?"

"You ask her."

"I dare you to do it."

When a man with a finely groomed mustache approached me, I assumed it would be with questions.

Instead, he slipped something into my hand.

Folded bills, as crisp as stationery.

He smiled, mustache turning up. "My wife would be simply thrilled if you could summon the apparition to our suite tomorrow evening."

Not long after that, a woman dressed as a firebird discreetly gave me a satin clutch. It was the size and shape of a croissant.

"Do you think if I gathered some of the girls together, you could arrange a midnight appearance?" she asked, eyes flashing like the cloth flames on her costume. "I promise we won't scare him."

When I had a moment alone to open the clutch, I found it filled with cash.

Later that night, a man in a Louis XIV–style ensemble, complete with white hose and a powdered wig, handed me a thick fold of bills. It was held together with a gold money clip.

"Let's have a chat and arrange a time for my lady and me to meet your ghost friend," he said, "shall we?"

It was as though the sky had opened, revealing a second Milky Way.

Paid appearances. Special fees for me to direct the ghost's activity. This was a whole new way for us to make money.

I now had enough cash on me that I was jumpy, eager to

bring it back to my room and hide it safely away. And maybe start penciling out how many appearances my brother might be able to do in a night.

"Where did McMonigle go?" I heard a man say as I passed a marble pillar.

"He went to deal with the fairy," another one said.

At the word *fairy*, I paused, my wings heavy on my back.

I peered around the pillar, watching the pair of young men who were talking. They were two of the men who'd been complaining about their inadequate allowances.

They were laughing, and while I listened for any repetition of the word *fairy*, they said a different word. An awful word. One that men sometimes called my brother for no reason except that he was attracted to other boys, and they could smell it on him, like he had crushed lavender in his pockets.

Fairy hadn't meant me. It had meant someone like my brother.

My brother had to take the blow of awful words both because he was brown and because he was gay. He took them quietly, stoically, never looking to the side, never giving anyone the satisfaction of his anger.

My brother had far more grace than I did.

I came around the pillar, throwing my head back and crying out in pain. "Oh!" I stretched out my hands toward the two young men. "What noxious airs accompany you!"

I was speaking loudly enough that every word gathered more attention.

"The whiff of death!" I shut my eyes, wincing. "The stench of evil!"

"Bixby, do something!" Blythe cried.

"I cannot bear it!" I went on. "The most horrible things

surround you. Ugly. Vile. Ghoulish." I made my voice weaker with every word. "They cling to you. They follow you. Simply hideous."

I was well practiced in the art of fake swooning. It was one of the first tricks I'd perfected, how to swirl and faint to the ground without injuring myself. My wings would only help cushion the fall.

Before I landed, someone caught me. In the same moment that Fairfax was yelling, "Get them out of here!" someone was slipping one arm under my wings and another under my knees. I let my head flop back, eyes still closed to keep up the act. But I wanted to know who had me and if I needed to get my claws out. I wanted to see the look on those men's faces. And I wanted to know what the dozen small thuds against the ground were; it sounded like someone had released a set of bouncing balls.

With my hair shielding my lolling head, I half opened my eyes.

I recognized Hayden's vest and trousers.

"Yes, bring her inside," I heard Blythe say. "Let her rest."

While the young men were complaining about being banished from the party—"On the word of a loon like her?"—Hayden was taking me down the stone steps into the lower garden. Through my half-open eyes, I saw the blur of round planets rolling down the steps ahead of us. They were bright amber, like Venus or Jupiter spinning through space.

I had never been close enough to Hayden to smell anything past the liquor and syrup-soaked cherries she worked with. But now that she was holding me like this, I could smell the things that left their scent on her. The flour-like starch she used on her pants and shirts. The aged paper of the book she was always carrying. Even the fresh but slightly metallic smell of the bicarbonate she must have used to brush her teeth.

The amber planets rolled down into the garden, slowing as they hit the grass.

Oranges. That had been the thudding noise. Hayden must have been carrying them and then dropped them to catch me.

Once I knew we were out of sight of the party, I lifted my head. "You can put me down now."

Hayden startled and lost her grip.

I hopped to my feet.

"You faked that?" Hayden was catching her breath.

I curtsied low like a stage actress during a curtain call.

Hayden's expression turned from annoyed shock to an amused smile. "You got those guys kicked out of that party on purpose."

I knelt on the chilled stone. "Maybe."

That slight smile bloomed full. "You were lying."

"I was not." I lifted the front of my skirt into a basket and gathered up the little Venuses and Jupiters. "Anyone who talks like that, who uses words like that, *does* have the stench of evil around him." I shrugged with one shoulder, one wing tilting. "I simply exaggerated their effect on me."

Hayden opened the burlap she had balled in her hand. "Here." Her fingers brushed my skirt as she lifted each orange planet from the green fabric, and I was suddenly annoyed that I had to give back this dress. I wanted to keep the paths that Hayden's fingers traced over this skirt. I wanted to keep the green sky from which Hayden's hands were lifting those amber planets. Since I'd arrived at The Coterie, this was the first thing I'd felt more sharply than the vines clinging to my skin.

Hayden looked at me, lips parted almost like she was

considering kissing me. And before I could really think about whether I wanted her to, I had a dozen questions, starting with: Wasn't she in love with someone else?

"You got the wrong one," Hayden said, voice low, looking down.

"What?" I asked.

"You guessed Iphis right." Hayden's eyes were back on my skirt and the oranges. "But there are two Iphises in *Metamorphoses*, and you picked the wrong one. I'm the other one."

LISANDRO

"I KNEW YOU were there." Embry gathered the clothes the man had knocked off the candelabras. "I could feel it." He looked up as though remembering something. "I'm Embry, by the way."

A flash of panic struck me. I hadn't come up with a name for myself. I hadn't needed to. Lola and I had never planned on me making small talk with anyone. If I was ever going to have a name, then Lola, the Magnificent Karina, would be the one to divine it.

"Ovidio," I said, my father's name falling off my tongue.

"Well, if there's anything I can do to return the favor, just say the word. I owe you." Embry looked up from gathering his shirts. "Is death really coming for him soon?"

"I'm afraid I don't know," I said. "Sorry to disappoint."

He smiled as he picked up the last of the hangers.

"Pardon my mess." Embry hooked each one back onto the candelabra arms. "I didn't realize I'd be having visitors."

I'd already inserted myself far more than I should have. Lola would wring my neck if I didn't take the opportunity to get a little information out of him.

"Why was that man going through your things?" I asked.

He gathered up scattered pencils. "Because my father thinks I've been stealing."

"Why?"

"Because things have been going missing." He set the pencils on the writing desk, the wood clicking as they settled. "And he couldn't imagine any of his guests stealing."

"But why blame you?" I asked.

"It's a long story. But better he blame me than anyone who works here." He neatened a sheaf of papers. "You know, I knew something was happening around here. Even before Blythe thought so." He tried to smooth a few crumpled sheets. "Weeks ago, I noticed this unfamiliar scent. I was catching it everywhere. I thought it might have been perfume, but it wasn't like anything any of the women here wear."

Weeks ago? The perfume was a classic trick of Lola's, but she wouldn't have had a chance to plant it until we got here.

"Sorry," he said. "I don't talk, and then I talk too much." He tilted his head a little as he shrugged, another one of those things that was like a hand on the back of my neck.

You never knew what could turn someone from just a person into someone you found intensely interesting. The cant of a boy's wrist as he pushed his hair off his face. The way a young businessman in a hotel lobby laughed when a pigeon fluttered onto his shoulder, his jokes about how he was now the most boring pirate known to man. How a boy at a produce stand bumped into me, grabbed my shoulder to steady me as he made his apologies, smiled as he walked away; if I hadn't been so set on making sure he hadn't picked my pocket, I might have smiled back.

I had a collection of such things, like worn stones I'd picked up off the beach. But with Embry Fairfax, they came faster and stranger than I was used to. I felt that shiver as he stacked papers, neatening the edges as gently as petting a cat. And again when he smoothed his eyebrow with his fourth finger. I couldn't figure out where the pool of my embarrassment was deepest: that I found Embry Fairfax attractive or that it was such odd things that were lighting the match.

"May I ask you something?" Embry said.

"Yes," I said, because *sure* or *okay* didn't sound archaic or ageless enough.

"The girl here," Embry said, "Is she a fraud?"

The chill at the back of my throat sank down into my chest.

Fraud. In our line of work, it was among the worst words you could hear. We were careful and good enough that we rarely did. Now I understood the hard-edged fear Lola must have felt when Hayden had said it.

"No," I said, flat, sure.

"Really?" Embry asked. "She's genuine?"

"Yes," I said, with all the calm conviction I could give the word.

"So she can help release you from here?" he asked.

"Yes," I said, as certain as the time before.

"Good. Then do whatever she says. Do whatever you need to do to get out of here." He picked up the glass jar full of leaves. "This place has a way of destroying people. Living and dead."

LOLA

I LAY ON my stomach on my bed, the night breeze from the open window turning pages for me.

Hayden had taught me something I either hadn't known or hadn't remembered: Ovid wrote about two characters named Iphis. I'd already found one of them, the shepherd who loved a princess. That princess scorned him with such gleeful ruthlessness that Aphrodite turned her to stone to match her heart.

Then there was the other Iphis, the one I'd missed.

The other Iphis was declared a girl at birth but, on the instruction of a goddess, was raised as a boy. Iphis grew up and was betrothed to a schoolmate, a girl named Ianthe. Iphis and Ianthe loved each other, and Ianthe couldn't wait for the wedding. Iphis, however, feared what would happen when Ianthe saw Iphis's body on their wedding night.

Iphis's mother tried to postpone the wedding in a series of increasingly ludicrous excuses. But eventually there was no more delaying. The date was set.

The night before the wedding, Iphis and his mother prayed desperately to that same goddess. The goddess looked kindly upon their humble devotion. She transformed Iphis's body into a male body, and the groom strode confidently toward his wedding.

Reading Iphis and Ianthe's story now was like my first time reading Song of Songs in Mamá's Biblia. It was so thrillingly beautiful that it seemed impossible I'd ever missed it. I should have seen it shining out from the middle of the book. And now that I knew it was there, all I wanted was to talk to someone else who saw it, too.

There were three kitchens at The Coterie, a fact I did not know until I visited every one of them looking for Hayden.

In the first, the cooks asked me a hundred questions about the haunting. I gave them secrets about where to avoid (if they didn't want to catch sight of the ghost) and where to linger (if they did). They showed me the secrets of their Welsh rarebit sauce, lending me a pencil and a recipe card so I could take down every word they said.

In the second, the bakers were polite but regarded me warily, as though my presence might stop their next day's bread dough from rising. I apologized for disturbing them and their bread dough.

The third was an auxiliary kitchen in an outbuilding, with a stone floor, a low ceiling, and a vast porcelain sink that seemed to take up half the space. Hayden was alone in there, washing a legion of glasses.

When I saw Hayden's back and shoulders leaning over the sink, when I remembered Hayden's fingers grazing my skirt, I lost the words I'd been carrying here with me. Everything felt either too trivial or too weighty to say out loud.

Hayden noticed me in the doorway and looked nervous. Tentative.

"Want a second?" I asked.

"Pardon?"

"A second?" I stepped toward the sink. "You know, like in a duel. You have your first swordsman, and then he brings his friend with him as a second swordsman. I thought you might want backup in your epic duel against those glasses."

Hayden's face relaxed. "Here." Hayden handed me a linen cloth. "I hate the drying more than the washing."

"Then you're in luck." I buffed the cloth over one of the damp glasses. "Water-spotting stemware was one of the first jobs I ever talked myself into."

"Oh yeah?" Hayden asked.

I nodded. "I was twelve, and even more adorable than I am now, if you can believe it, and I convinced a hotel kitchen manager that he'd be doing me a great charity and his accounting books a great favor since I offered my services so cheaply."

"Not as cheaply as I'm getting them," Hayden said.

"Touché, good sir."

Like so many things I said, it had just come out. And as soon as said it, I wondered if I'd overstepped.

"May I ask you something?" I said.

Hayden nodded.

"I'm not trying to be nosy. I just want to get something right in my head."

Hayden's posture stiffened. A patch of lemon pith on a glass became the focal point of Hayden's universe.

But how could I get anything right if I didn't ask?

"Is that your favorite story in *Metamorphoses* because you like girls or because you're a boy?" I asked.

"Yes," Hayden said, fast, getting it over with. "Both."

I cringed. I should have listed *both* as an option.

"Does that"—Hayden looked at me—"Are you"—and then at the tiled wall in front of us—"Do either or both of those things make you want to run screaming from the room?"

"No," I said. "Not at all. I just feel a little stupid."

"Why?" Hayden asked.

"Because there are some of those stories I know so well," I said.

Growing up, I'd wanted to tame a stag like Cyparissus, sure I'd be a gentler, more careful hunter than he was. Apollo's love for the prince Hyacinthus was so passionate that I wanted to steal Ovid's stylus and write them a happier ending. I'd stayed awake at night wondering if Galatea, the statue Pygmalion had wished to life, got to decide if she even wanted to be with him. Maybe once she stepped off her pedestal, she wanted the chance to see the world for herself.

"And because I know some of them so well," I said, "sometimes I assume I know the whole book, even though I know I don't. Clearly. I didn't even remember there were two Iphises."

"It's okay," Hayden said.

His hands dipped in and out of the soapy water.

"You know, it's not a perfect story," he said. "Iphis laments the love between them as being monstrous, and it's not as though anyone corrects Iphis on that. The story only gets resolved by Iphis being physically and magically transformed into being male."

Our fingers brushed as Hayden handed me a heavy crystal glass. His hands smelled like lemon and soap, and the fizzing in my chest got so loud that I couldn't keep looking at him.

I eased the glass into the linen cloth. We returned our eyes to our respective tasks.

"After I read it about a hundred times," Hayden said, "after the thrill of it lost its sheen a little, I wondered about that. How much of it was relief over being transformed into what you really always were, and how much of it was relief because if Iphis wasn't transformed, Ianthe might have rejected him?"

"Yeah." I added a perfectly spotless glass—if I did say so myself—to the growing rows on the counter. "That part seemed so lonely to me."

"What do you mean, lonely?" Hayden asked.

"Do they ever even talk about it?" I asked. "Does Iphis ever know if Ianthe would have been in love either way? Does Iphis ever get to know if the body he had when he and Ianthe fell in love is one Ianthe would have loved, too? Or does he just have to live with all that alone?"

Hayden paused, looking at me. I hadn't seen this kind of openness in his face before. It wasn't just relief. It was surprise.

Then he flinched, like he was coming back from a day-dream. He smiled as he turned over the next glass. "You ask a lot of questions."

"I know," I said.

"But a lot of them are really good ones." He handed me a washed champagne flute. "I still love that story. Because even with all that, that story saw me. Pages in a book understood me more than anyone else ever had."

I watched Hayden's hands in the water, the sleeves of his shirt cuffed up to his elbows.

"So how about you?" he asked. "Why do you like *Metamorphoses* so much?"

"My father used to read the stories to us all the time," I said. "Well, not all of them. Some of them he either edited or edited out because of our age."

"Who's us?" Hayden asked.

Mierda.

I'd slipped.

Too late now. Time for some improvisation.

"My brother and me," I said.

"You have a brother?" Hayden asked.

Time for a terrific lie.

"An older brother," I said. "He's a priest."

With as pious and reverent of a spiritualist as he'd played, that was practically the truth.

Hayden eyed me. "A priest?"

"Yes. The whole family's very proud of him."

"Your brother's a priest, and you commune with ghosts?"

"We're Mexican," I said. "It all goes together better than you might think. In fact, we often seek each other's counsel on matters in our professions. It's very useful to have a priest in the family. Like a doctor, but for your soul."

Hayden laughed. "I can see that."

"How old were you?" I asked. "When you first read Iphis and Ianthe?"

"About the age you were when you were talking hotel managers into giving you jobs," Hayden said. "Even before I found Iphis and Ianthe, though, I read the book because of all those stories about becoming something else. It gave me hope even before I knew for sure what I wanted to become."

I took a highball glass from Hayden, the soap bubbles on his hands like sea-foam.

"Do you think it ever happens like that?" he asked. "People becoming something else?"

My body was proof that it happened. I was becoming a tree of a girl, from the inside out. Even if I succeeded at The Coterie, even if I dodged the fates of Daphne or Diopatre's sisters, I would be a girl who became part tree and then became a girl again. This becoming and unbecoming would always be part of my body.

"My mother certainly thought so," I said. "I grew up on stories of lovers becoming volcanoes. People turning to ocelots and back. She made me paint my feet with iodine when I went out barefoot because she told me if I didn't, evil spirits could transform me into mushrooms."

"My mother told me that if I ever stuck my tongue out at her behind her back, I'd turn into a gecko," Hayden said.

"See? You know exactly what I'm talking about." I eyed him. "So did you ever test it?"

He shrugged. "I'm not a lizard yet."

We were quiet as we fell back into the rhythm of our tasks. I didn't mind it so much. I wasn't used to not minding quiet.

"Do you think it could happen to me?" Hayden asked.

"Well, if you're not catching flies yet . . . ," I said.

"Not that," he said. "Do you think what happened to Iphis in the story could happen to me?"

Hayden looked at me with such earnest hope that I wished I were a goddess who could make it happen for him. I wanted to give him everything Iphis got in the story, everything the pages named. Not just the changes in body, but also the swagger that came with being a boy. That was the thing about Iphis's transformation. The story mentioned his *stride* because the way he walked made as much of a difference as the new muscles he walked with. The *audacious* way he spoke mattered as much as the lowering of his voice. His features hadn't just changed; he was *embolden'd with an awful grace.* The way he took up space in the world transformed him as much as his body.

Then I remembered the line about Iphis's instantaneous goddess-given haircut. *Long hair to curling locks withdrew.* The haircut was the thing Iphis could have most easily managed on his own. He hadn't even given himself that one small part of what he wanted. Something had held him back.

Hayden had a haircut that was short and daring, but it was still a woman's haircut. Hayden wore masculine clothes, but they were still women's clothes.

"You've never thought about making it happen yourself?" I asked.

"Of course I have." Hayden stirred the water, fluffing up soap bubbles. "But I always get stuck on the clothing."

"*That's* where you get stuck?" I asked.

"Don't look at me like that. I don't study catalogs like they're textbooks. We're not all girls used to wearing evening gowns."

If only he knew who I'd been before I was the Magnificent Karina.

"I get stuck on it because what if I don't fit?" Hayden asked.

"Then you try a different size."

"Not what if *they* don't fit. What if *I* don't fit?" he asked. "What if I try wearing men's clothing and it's wrong, and I'm not any good at being a man? What if I can't wear it right? As long as I don't try it, I don't have to know. I haven't even figured out my name. Hayden's my last name, and I like it that way, so that's as far as I've gotten."

He handed me the last flute in the sink.

"When you do know your name," I said as I dried it, "will you tell me?"

Hayden nodded.

"Good night, Karina," he said as we closed up the kitchen.

That was when I did something more reckless than any bar fight, any impulsive theft, any insult that left my mouth before I could stop it.

"Lola," I said.

"What?" Hayden asked.

If I wanted his name, how could I not offer mine?

"It's a secret," I said, "but 'Karina' is just as much of a professional name as 'Magnificent' is. My family calls me Lola."

Hayden smiled, and it was as soft as the garden lamps glowing through the windows. "Lola," he repeated, and in his mouth it became a new name. It became something glimmering, and I wanted to wear it like a jewel.

That night, while the guests were taking one another's money over games of bassette, I sneaked into the rooms of the young men I liked the least. I went from one to the next, turning through their things like flipping pages in a book.

When I'd stuffed my canvas bag full, I declared my work done.

"There you are."

At the sound of Bixby Fairfax's voice, I froze in the hallway.

I briefly considered whether I could hide this monstrosity of a bag behind my back. I briefly considered whether I could run and pretend I hadn't heard him. I briefly considered whether I could brain him with a heavy book and later convince him that it had fallen from a high shelf.

I turned slowly, weighed down with dread.

"That was very quick action tonight, young lady." There was no accusation in his face. He was beaming. "I wish half the men I hired at my companies were as ready on their feet."

"The same gifts that allow me to sense spirits sometimes allow me to sense other shifts in the air." I gave a modest dip of my head. "On occasion I can tell when a storm is coming before the meteorologists." I was rambling now.

"Fascinating," he said, his expression far off, musing.

Then his eyes landed on the canvas in my arms.

The bag suddenly felt as heavy as if I'd stuffed it with stones from the garden.

"You know they'll come get your laundry for you," Fairfax said.

"I have a few stains I've been neglecting." I smiled, hoping I wasn't overdoing it. "One of your guests kindly offered to show me a few tricks. I wish I could remember her name"—I made a show of trying—"but I know my way to her room."

"The staff will gladly see to any stains for you," he said.

"Oh, but I do like to learn a few secrets of housekeeping," I said. "A lady can never have too many domestic skills, can she?"

Fairfax leaned in as though we were conspiring. The smell of a recent cigar wafted between us. "Perhaps you could be a good influence on my Blythe."

I forced the appropriate laughter, light and brief.

"And speaking of skills," Fairfax said, "I hear you're even more of a gifted young lady than we thought."

"I'm sorry?" I asked.

"Summoning a ghost to specific rooms?" A grin lit his entire face. "Why didn't you mention that little talent before?" He wedged a folded stack of bills between my fingers and the canvas bag. It was even thicker and heavier than the ones I'd been given at the costume ball.

"Completely apart from your fee, of course." Fairfax waved his hand in a reassuring gesture. "Consider it a gift for doing me a special favor."

"I'm afraid I don't understand," I said.

"It's very simple," he said. "All you need to do is send the ghost to the Venetian Suite. Sometime over the next couple of days. In fact, don't do it tonight. He might be expecting it. And the closer to the middle of the night, the better." He looked as animated as during the height of the costume ball. "Three or four in the morning."

"You want the ghost to wake someone up?" I asked.

"Exactly." Fairfax jabbed a finger in the air. "I have a score to settle."

I held the bag tighter against me, dampening the twist in my stomach.

Fairfax wanted me to do his bidding. He wanted me to frighten a rival or someone he thought had wronged him. He either didn't have the nerve to kick someone out of The Coterie, or he found more satisfaction in keeping him around and harassing him.

"Scare the daylights out of him." Fairfax was already walking away, throwing words and a jovial laugh back over his shoulder. "Put the fear of God in him."

"I'll see what I can do," I said, my smile so polite it sugared my voice.

For now, I would do anything Fairfax asked of me. I would

do anything that would earn me his trust. And by the time I turned everything against him, there would be no stopping me. By the time I turned on him, on Blythe, on everyone, I would have my fingers so deep into the ground here that no one could pull me out by the roots.

LISANDRO

"SO YOU'RE HERE at eleven." Over breakfast, Lola traced her pencil across my sketched map of The Coterie.

"Right," I said. It came out flat. Whatever mood my sister was in lately, I was giving it as little fuel as I could.

"And then here and here around midnight, roughly," she went on.

"Understood," I said.

"And then you're probably avoiding coming back here because you probably hate your sister, because your sister is meaner than a weasel," she said.

I looked up from the map.

"I'm sorry," Lola said. "It was a terrible thing for me to say, and I didn't mean it, and no matter what I think of Embry Fairfax, that's no excuse to say anything like what I said. Hence my status as weasel of a sister."

"That's not fair," I said.

She looked worried.

I tried to hold off my smile. "You're not *quite* as mean as a weasel."

Now she was smiling. "No?"

"In my heart, you're solidly a ferret," I said.

"I'll take it." She pointed back at the map. "Oh, and then you're over here at about three, three thirty in the morning."

"Three thirty in the morning?" I said.

"Don't ask." She sipped her tea, her expression one of summoning her patience.

"Wouldn't it be easier for me to just appear to everyone at once?" I asked.

"All in good time." Lola was inhaling the rest of her pain aux raisins. "Now wish me luck. The lady of the house has requested that I help her rehearse her lines for her next picture." She blotted her napkin against her mouth. "So I get to spend the day hearing Blythe's rendition of Mary, Queen of Scots."

I cringed. "Heaven have mercy on her soul and yours."

"From your lips to God's ears." Lola sat on the sofa, buckling her shoes. "I think she's genuinely hoping I'll hear acting advice from the deceased queen herself."

I stirred a spoon through my tea even though I didn't take cream or sugar—a nervous habit. It was what I did instead of telling my sister where I was going.

When I got to the back of Embry's mirror, I could hear a faint whispering on the other side of the wall.

Embry was flicking a pencil across pieces of cardboard. They were scattered around like playing cards.

"Hi," he said when he noticed me. He sounded surprised, but something about the breath under the word was like a window opening, like he was making space in the room for me.

"I just wanted to make sure you were all right," I said. "And that you didn't need anyone else scared off."

He smiled, dipping his head so his hair shadowed his face. "Not so far, thankfully."

He guided the pencil in those perfect circles, his grip loose and open.

"What are you drawing?" I asked.

"I'm trying to work out a modified electrical circuit." He held up what was now a series of penciled circles and connecting lines. "It's based off a selenium sensor. A photosensitive circuit. Darkness closes the circuit, so the lamp turns on. Light interrupts the circuit, so the lamp turns off."

"Do you always work out electrical problems on cardboard?" I asked.

"It's from the cigarette cartons." He turned the cardboard over, showing the red and green of a logo. "The guests here smoke like chimneys, and all those cartons are such waste I thought why not take them as drawing paper?"

He was such an odd contrast to the excess of The Coterie. The thrift of him didn't fit with the place. Even his shirt had the well-worn look of a favorite.

"I'm glad you're here," he said. "I was hoping I'd see you again before the Magnificent Karina sent you on your way."

He looked so genuinely and earnestly happy to see me that I felt compelled to correct him, to remind him of the truth even if that truth was a lie.

"I'm not really here," I said. "Not in the way you are. You know that, right?"

"I know," he said.

"Then why were you hoping you'd see me again?"

Embry paused, studying the silver lines in front of him. "When we see the stars, we're seeing light from thousands of years ago. It doesn't make it any less real than the light from a lamp across the room. It just takes longer to get to us. You're here as much as I am. The only difference is that I'm made of molecules and you're made of light. Energy versus matter. And each can become the other, so how different can they be?"

It was so unexpected, the flicker inside me, that my body remembered I wasn't as dead as I pretended to be.

I paused, working up to the question I'd come to ask. "What did you mean when you said I should leave here as soon as I can? What did you mean when you said this place destroys people?"

The tips of his fingers reddened, choking up on the lead.

"The other ghost," he said.

When I was quiet, he looked up, expectant.

When I stayed quiet, he said, "I saw her three, maybe four times. And I'm not the only one. But she was here, and then she wasn't. It was like she disappeared. Evaporated. And I don't think it's because she's somehow okay and simply moved on. Nothing around here seems okay."

The ghost girl.

The rumor that would not die.

"I thought maybe you knew her." Embry lowered his eyes again. "But I guess, now that I think about it, that's pretty offensive, isn't it?"

"Why would that be offensive?" I couldn't help having a little fun with him. He was so serious about a haunting that existed even less than I did. “Because you thought all ghosts know each other?”

He flushed without any trace of laughter. “Because I thought maybe she looked Mexican.” He closed his eyes, cringing with embarrassment. “I thought she even looked a little like you.”

LISANDRO

WHEN I OPENED the door to our rooms, Lola was messing with something in her wardrobe. The moment she saw me, she shoved it all back in and shut the doors. As though I didn't already know that her dresses were stolen from the Magnificent Karina.

As though everything she hadn't told me might be on hangers, among all those layers of tulle.

"What are you doing here?" Lola's smile looked as brittle as stale pastry. "Don't you have a ghostly appointment in—" She tried to look past me at the clock.

"Maybe," I said. "Or maybe you do."

For the first time since I'd walked in, her expression looked genuine. It was pure confusion.

"I'm going to ask this once." I stood in the doorway to her room. "If you tell me there's nothing to it, I'll believe you. But please don't lie to me."

She looked suddenly unsteady, as though the carpet were buckling under her.

"Did you prehaunt this place?" I asked.

I didn't know if it was the relief of the truth being spoken out loud between us or if she was just pleased with herself. But I could tell, instantly, that she was trying not to smile.

"Oh, please tell me you didn't," I said.

She was losing the fight with her own face.

"Lola!" I couldn't raise my voice. I couldn't risk us being heard through these flimsy walls. So I ended up doing something just above whisper-yelling. "What would you have done if you'd gotten caught?"

"But I didn't," she said.

"I cannot believe this is funny to you."

"It's only funny because ghost-me is yesterday's news." She pushed past me into the sitting area. "Ghost-you is all the latest."

"No." I turned around to face her. "Ghost-you is not yesterday's news. People are still talking about ghost-you."

She paused mid-step. "What?"

"Yeah." I leaned against the doorframe, hard, like I could transfer my frustration from my shoulder into the wood. "You were apparently quite memorable. In your signature white dress. And to think I thought I was the first one who got to see your jilted bride act."

"I did not do my jilted bride act here," Lola said. "There was no veil involved. You know I don't recycle backstories."

"I really should have known something was up when they were talking about that perfume wafting around here," I said. "I know that's one of your favorite tricks. But I thought that was the power of suggestibility, that you'd done it so well they'd backdated it to before we got here. No wonder you've been so jumpy lately."

"It's okay." Lola had her eyes closed, her hands patting the air on either side of her. "We can fix this. We're going to fix this."

"'We'?" I asked. "How can *we* do anything when you're keeping things from me?"

Her eyes snapped open. "I kept it from you because I knew you wouldn't want me to do it."

"Of course I wouldn't," I said. "Because this is a spectacularly bad idea."

"Was." She pointed at the air between us. "*Was* a spectacularly bad idea. But we're getting away with it."

"Do you know how much more complicated this makes everything?" I asked. "As if it wasn't complicated enough. What if the guests keep talking about ghost-you and Blythe and Fairfax think ghost-you needs to be banished, too? How are you going to do that? If you know a lighting trick that can make two of you, you certainly haven't shared it with me."

"And if we need to figure one out, we will," she said.

"Really?" I asked. "Just like that? That easy?"

"I don't think you're understanding me." She grabbed her handbag off a nearby chair. "So let me give you a little illustration." She opened the clasp and showed it to me.

It was stuffed with more cash than I'd ever seen in one place.

"Please"—was the first word I managed to get out—"for the love of all that is holy"—I stared into the maw of that bag—"tell me you did not steal this."

"Not a penny." She shut the clasp. "Do you want to know why you're going all over the resort? Because guests are paying me to specifically summon you to their rooms." She threw the bag at me.

I caught it in midair before it could knock into a lamp.

"You're the status symbol of the season," Lola said. "You're even better than a couture gown or a designer shoe."

"Well, if I'm better than a shoe, that fixes everything, doesn't it?"

"Will you listen for one second?" she asked. "I've been thinking this through. Everyone wants to feel special. Everyone wants to be able to say they've seen you in their own personal apparition. As soon as we show you off during a party or a cocktail hour, we cheapen you."

"Wow, thanks," I said.

"Don't you get it?" Lola asked. "The more exclusive we make you, the more ghost-me becomes old news. Last season's fashions. Plus, the more we do this, the more money we walk away with."

I set Lola's handbag on a chair. It was so heavy it seemed like it needed a whole seat of its own.

Lola had found us an unexpected income stream. If we kept this up, we'd not only be able to set ourselves up in New York, San Francisco, Chicago. We'd be able to pay our rent months in advance. Lola could enroll at any acting school she wanted.

I'd wanted somewhere there were other people like me, to find those secret spaces where I could be who I was without looking over my shoulder. I could have that, and Lola could have a better life than I ever thought I could give her.

"This is working," she said. "Don't you see that?"

She had still lied to me. We were an act, my sister and I, and she had lied to me.

"Is this what you wanted the whole time?" I asked. "For us to steal the Magnificent Karina's act? Was that part of your whole strategy?"

"Of course not." Shock and offense muddled on Lola's face so quickly that I knew she was telling the truth. "When she showed up in the hotel lobby, I wanted to tear her limb from limb. *I* was supposed to be the ghost here." She stabbed her painted fingernail toward her sternum. "This was supposed to be my best spectral performance yet. Do you think I wanted to be stuck playing her? I hate her!"

"You don't hate her," I said. "You hate that she got in our way. You hate that she messed with our plans."

"No, I hate her." Lola went to the writing desk. "I actually hate her." She opened a drawer and dug out a book with gold-edged pages. "Meet Margaret Drummond."

"Who?" I asked.

"Otherwise known as the Magnificent Karina." Lola sank into the sitting-area sofa.

"How do you know that?" I asked.

"Because that's her diary," Lola said. "And you know what I learned about Margaret Drummond? She doesn't need money. She never did. Apparently the Drummonds are very prominent in Cape Cod society. She's a bored, obscure socialite who wasn't making the splash she wanted to. Her debutante ball with her stupid blue-blood roses was her high point. It was all downhill after that. So she made herself into someone else, someone people would remember."

I studied the inscription inside the front cover, the name in elegant penmanship.

"All she wants is to be adored." Lola leaned back on the

sofa, staring at the ceiling. "Revered. Sought after. And guess what? She's willing to do anything. Including getting money out of heartbroken families."

At those words, the diary felt like poison in my hands. It would turn to liquid. It would eat through the carpet underneath me.

Lola gestured at my expression. "My thoughts exactly. You can read all about it in there. She practically gloats. She tells people who've lost loved ones that she can connect them again. She does exactly what—" Her voice frayed, and she lost the end of the sentence.

She didn't need to finish it. I knew.

The Magnificent Karina did to grieving families exactly what a con artist once did to us.

I waited for the tightness in my throat to ease.

"I'm sorry," Lola said. "I know I should have told you about everything from the beginning. But I knew how long we'd both dreamed about getting out of here, getting something better than all those small jobs. And I knew we'd need money, so I wanted us to run a job up here. And when you said what you said about us needing a reputation, I knew we needed it even more."

My guilt was as annoying and unsettling as a hornet's buzzing. Lola had wanted this as much for me as for herself.

"So when the Magnificent Karina showed up, I couldn't let it go," Lola said. "This is our chance. Please don't let my mistakes get in the way of that."

Lola could see that life, too, the glitter of city lights, the secret parties, the chances to play a hundred different roles instead of a hundred different variations on ghost girl.

It was a glint of possibility in her eyes as she stared at the far wall.

Getting somewhere better was my dream. Getting to something better was Lola's.

I set down the chronicles of Margaret Drummond.

"No more stupid risks." I sat down next to Lola. "Okay?"

Lola straightened up, hopeful, nodding. "None at all. I promise."

LOLA

THE GHOST GIRL I'd been was coming back to haunt me.

I needed to know just how much of a problem she might turn out to be. And if there was anyone who heard everything in a place like this, it was the guy pouring the drinks.

The hillside brush whispered under Hayden's steps. "Remind me why we're out here?"

"I can't remind you." I smiled over my shoulder. "I haven't told you yet."

My dress, as violet as a crocus, streamed across the space between us every time the wind picked up. This fabric looked so spectacular in moonlight I almost wanted to pen a letter of thanks to Margaret Drummond.

"You know there are coyotes around here, right?" Hayden asked.

I lifted the hem of my skirt for a patch of rocky ground. "But at least the snakes are sleeping."

"Not the night snakes," Hayden said.

I froze.

"Nobody told you about the night snakes?" Hayden asked.

I slowly looked over my shoulder.

Hayden was grinning, waiting for the joke to land.

I kept walking. "You're horrible."

"Thank you," he said. "I do try."

As we moved farther down the slope, away from the landscaped grounds, the shadows of oak trees grew closer. With every flicker of movement in their silhouetted branches, I remembered Mamá's stories about birds that appeared only on moonless nights. Lisandro and I used to sneak outside to look for them, swearing we could feel their feathers brushing our backs in the dark.

"Now that you've scared me half to death, the least you can do is give your opinion on something," I said. "Have you heard any talk about the spirit of a young woman around here? Has anyone seen anything?"

"Drunk people think they see everything," Hayden said. "Are you really not going to tell me what we're doing out here?"

We passed under the canopy of an oak grove. The trees grew in an uneven ring, and their boughs wove lace out of overlapping shadows.

"That bag you're carrying looks too light for weapons," Hayden said, "so I do find some comfort there."

"About that." As my eyes adjusted, a second veil of lace came into focus, a sprinkling of moonlight through the leaves. "I brought you a few things." I opened the bag to show him. "And you're out here in the dark, so if you don't like how it feels, no one has to see. I don't have to see. Even you don't have to see. And if it doesn't feel right and you need someone to blame, you can blame me instead of blaming yourself."

Hayden looked at the clothes in the canvas laundry bag. "Where did you get these?"

"The less you know, the better," I said.

"How do you even know these'll fit me?" he asked.

"Trust me," I said. "I know clothes. They'll fit you. At least enough to give you a feel for them."

Hayden swore under his breath.

"What?" I asked. "You have an objection to wing collars?"

He looked up. "You stole these."

"What did I just say?" I asked. "The less you know, the better."

"You stole these from guests, didn't you?" Hayden said, a breathless, disbelieving laugh under his words.

"Only the ones who've really gotten on my bad side," I said. "Besides, they each have acres of clothing. I'll bet you a week of washing glasses that none of them even notices. They don't care about what they have. All they care about is acquiring what they don't have. So in that spirit, I think it's only fitting that I acquire a few things for you."

"I could get fired for this," Hayden said.

"No one's going to find out."

"If they find any of these in my room, I'll look like a thief. They'll have me arrested."

"Do you think I didn't think of that?" I asked. "I'll keep them in my room for you."

Hayden's posture seemed to calm. Slightly.

"If you tell me I'm overstepping," I said, "we'll go right back up that hill right now. But if we do, let it be because you're telling me this is none of my business and that you hate that I did this, not because you don't think you deserve it. And definitely not because you think you deserve it less than any of those pendejos up there."

Maybe my eyes were still adjusting. Maybe I was seeing what I wanted to see in the low light. But Hayden looked like he was considering it.

"And if I hate this," he said, "we can pretend it never happened?"

I looked around, turning my head every which way. "Pretend what never happened?"

Hayden let me transfer the bag into his arms.

"They're folded into outfits," I said. "If you don't like one of them, or any of them, you don't even have to show me." I put my back against the wide trunk of one of the oaks. "I'll be here. I won't look."

Hayden went around the same tree.

"So why are you asking about the girl in the gardens?" Hayden said from the other side.

"Who?" I asked.

"That's what I've mostly heard her called," Hayden said. "The girl in the gardens."

"So she does exist."

"Shouldn't you know that better than I do?"

"Therein lies my dilemma," I said. "I mostly hear about the spirit of the young man wandering the building at night. You saw him out in the gardens, same as I did, but ever since, he's been within the walls of the house." Sometimes behind them. "Yet I hear the occasional whisper about the ghost of a young woman who's apparently only ever been seen outside. So my quandary is, do I concentrate my energies inside the building, so as to further my work with the young man, or outside, so as to determine if there's any credence to the stories about the girl?"

"You've seen one ghost yourself," Hayden said. "You've never seen the other. And you're going to redirect your efforts on the word of a few very—and I know this because I'm the one serving them—intoxicated guests?"

"I know," I said. "But my work requires open-mindedness. The problem is I'm not usually dealing with this many people, this many opinions at once. Sometimes even I can't tell what's something that was truly witnessed, what's rumor, what people think they've seen because they're afraid to see it, what people convince themselves they've seen because they want to have seen it. The human mind is very suggestible."

I said it as though it was something that made my work difficult instead of something that made my work possible.

Lisandro was right. I should have told him about all of this from the beginning. Then we could have figured out our strategy earlier. We could have already worked out what to do about any hint of rumor regarding a ghostly girl. Ignore them? Stage a scene in which ghost-Lisandro denounced her as a delusion? Make another story out of her, one good enough to explain her disappearance? Write Lisandro a grand speech about how he himself had driven her away?

After a few more seconds of rustling fabric, Hayden's voice came around the tree. "So what was the one about the volcanoes?"

"What?" I asked.

"The story you mentioned," he said, "about the lovers turning into volcanoes. That's not in *Metamorphoses*, is it?"

"No," I said. "That's a Nahuatl love story. There are a lot of versions of it, but this is the one my mother told me: A princess fell in love with a warrior against the wishes of her parents. Her father had him sent into battle, and though the princess feared for his life, the warrior welcomed the opportunity to prove himself worthy of her hand in marriage. But then a false report came back from the battle that the warrior had been killed."

My vision readjusted, and I noticed that the trees here weren't all the same. They weren't all live oaks. Some had thinner silhouettes like young ash trees. Taller shoulders like elms. The wide, bushy spreads of walnuts. The silver tint of olive leaves.

The whispering of fabric pulled me back to the story.

"The princess died of a broken heart." I could almost hear Mamá's voice overlapping with my own. "Her broken heart turned to ice. Her flesh turned to snow. When her warrior love returned home and he saw what had happened, he lay down beside her and died of his own grief, his love still smoldering in his heart like a torch. The gods were so touched by their devotion to each other that they transformed the lovers into a snow-covered mountain and a still-smoking volcano, so that the land bore monuments to their enduring love."

I waited for the inevitable *That's depressing*. Or *That's it? That's how it ends?*

But the next words from the other side of the tree were "That's beautiful. Sad but beautiful."

Hayden couldn't see me smiling, but I liked thinking that maybe Mamá could.

"That's what I always thought," I said.

As the branches shifted, the moon glanced off patches of the other tree trunks. Something shiny, like the inside of a shell, caught the light.

"I'm not looking," I said as I stepped toward the other trees. "I'm just walking around."

"I believe you," Hayden said.

I went close enough to see the textures. There were sprinklings of smooth spots, like tiles. There were lacquered, pale contours like miniature carvings in marble.

They looked like fingernails growing out of the bark. They looked so much like teeth pushing up from under the wood that fear and wonder hitched in my chest.

I didn't touch the teeth or the fingernails. But the second my hand grazed the bark, the nails drew back, retracting. The teeth sank into the wood and vanished. It happened so fast it looked like scattering, nothing more than moths and beetles flittering across the trees.

"Okay," Hayden said behind me.

I turned around.

Every time I'd ever altered an old, cast-off skirt to make it flatter me, I'd glittered with pride. Every time I'd taken in a secondhand shirt so that it fit Lisandro properly, I was bringing my brother into focus. Every time I'd added beading or embroidery to make a dress look more expensive, I was scattering stardust.

None of it came close to this.

Hayden's posture was tentative, questioning. But he was standing with his weight rooted in the ground. He looked like he was claiming the gravity between his body and the earth.

Maybe, sometimes, that was what it took. Trousers that were cut in men's style. A shirt that buttoned the direction men's shirts buttoned. Hayden hadn't even put on the tie, but he looked as pulled together as any of the men I'd stolen these clothes from. He belonged in them better. Sometimes to show up to your own life, you had to show up in the right clothes. Sometimes to show up as who you truly were, you needed the right costume.

"How do I look?" Hayden gave me an exaggerated shrug. "Audacious? Sparkling with manly vigor?"

I crossed the brush toward him. "Don't joke."

"I have to joke so I don't feel like a joke."

"You're not," I said. "And you look like who you are; that's how you look." I pulled at the lapels. "Now stay there. We need the finishing touches."

Hayden's shoulders relaxed enough for me to make sure the shirt and the jacket were sitting the way they should. I looped the satin band of a tie, as green as a billiard table, under the back of his collar.

Beneath the starched fabric, his shirt was as thin as writing paper. I could feel the muscles in his neck. I didn't realize how long my fingers had paused there until he closed his eyes.

"Sorry," I said.

He shook his head, a wordless *Don't worry about it.*

"I didn't steal you an evening coat," I said as I tied the four-in-hand knot, "because tails don't look good on anyone unless they're fitted perfectly around the waist and shoulders."

"That," Hayden said, "and I've never in my life had occasion to wear tails to anything."

"Details, details." I adjusted the knot into place.

Hayden looked as handsome as any man who'd ever sauntered into The Coterie. I had truly done the Lord's work. Good clothes belonged on good men. Not men who called boys like my brother awful names and then slept easily at night, their own names embroidered into nightshirts and satin bathrobes. They considered men who liked men too soft, yet they refused to travel anywhere without their Marseilles waistcoats and their silk undergarments. They saw something lacking in boys like my brother, yet they insisted they simply could not live without a different suit for every day of the year. These were the men who declared themselves arbiters of all masculinity, when there was nothing holding up their own except for their money.

Maybe before we left, I'd steal my brother a new wardrobe, too.

Hayden's look was almost perfect, but not quite. Something was off, a mismatch in line and form.

"Can I touch your hair?" I asked Hayden.

"Sure," he said.

He had that haircut that had once made me think he was intimidatingly fashionable. Middle part. Just long enough to tuck behind his ears. Blunt cut touched up so recently it had sharp edges, as slick as black glass. It looked good on him. But now that I was seeing him in men's-cut clothing, the geometry didn't work quite as well. It was like how the dress I wore determined whether I pinned my hair up or kept it down.

"And by touch your hair, I mean mess it up," I said.

"I figured."

I brushed it forward with my fingers and into his face. I was trying to get an idea of how it would look if some of it fell onto his forehead.

"What's the verdict?" he asked. "Do I look more handsome with more of my face covered?"

"No, and you're interfering with my concentration," I said.

"Sorry."

I slipped my hands into his hair and combed it back with my fingers. "You have a very nice forehead."

"Surely the weirdest compliment I've ever gotten," he said.

"You're welcome." A few locks of his hair had gotten loose from the comb of my fingers, so I moved one of my hands to fix them. Whether it was an outfit or a lighting configuration, I wanted things exactly right. In matters of both fashion and deception, details were everything.

My fingers brushed his forehead, and he closed his eyes again.

I could have pretended that this was the first time I'd thought of how my mouth would feel against his. I could have blamed it on the way he tilted his head forward, his lips parted like my hands in his hair was the most calming and the most thrilling thing he'd ever felt. I could have kissed him and pretended it had just happened, spur of the moment.

But everything I could lose was buzzing through my head. Every lie I had told Hayden, every secret I had kept from Lisandro, hummed in the air. The vines twisting along my skin, the wooden knobs of my spine, made me feel like my blood and bones were on the outside of my body.

"Could I ask you something?" I said.

"Anything," he said, so fast there was no air between my voice and his.

I'd grown up hearing myths where the ground revealed the truth. Dill sprang up, warning an innocent heart of a lover's vanity. An oak and a linden next to each other marked a place of safety, concealed from enemies. A sudden flowering of mint revealed an act of treachery.

If I kissed Hayden, the ground would not burst into a thousand violet flowers. It would twist into thorns and brambles, warning him of what I really was.

The worst thing you could do during a job was care about

someone. It muddled your thinking. It meant you gave a little of your power to someone else, when what I needed to do was clamp my hands around every bit I had.

"If you hear anything else about the ghost girl," I said, "will you let me know?"

Hayden's jaw tensed. A sad, cynical smile curved his mouth, and he held a small, bitter laugh at the back of his throat.

"Yeah." He took a step back. "Sure." He kept pulling back. "I'll let you know."

The way he held his shoulders and his limbs was just like a man. But I couldn't even tell him this, not without it seeming like a move on a chessboard.

"Hayden," I said.

"Don't worry." He held up a hand, barely pausing as he walked away. "We're fine."

With a few words, I'd turned everything between us into an exchange of currency. I'd closed my hands tight enough not to give anything up, and my curled fists had crushed it all to dust.

LOLA

THE NEXT NIGHT, Blythe ordered the terraces transformed into a Parisian street scene, complete with lampposts, café tables, twinkling lights, fabric awnings. From the staircases that wrapped around the mansion's exterior, it looked like an illuminated town square had sprung up in the dark.

I dressed to the theme. Cloche hat. The shortest and chicest of the Magnificent Karina's coats. T-strap shoes I'd freshly polished. And I hoped every detail would hide how little I wanted to go to this party.

I'd hurt Hayden. I'd lied to my brother when he'd given me the perfect chance to tell him the whole truth. And in my sleep, I tried to claw the vines off my legs and the trunk of my spine off my own back. I put cracks in everything I touched, from my own body to the hearts of boys I cared about.

As I was crossing a stair landing, the sound of Fairfax's voice made me pause. It rose from the lower gardens.

Fairfax sounded annoyed, my cue to stay away. It was best to be out of his field of vision when he was annoyed. He'd sent guests home on a whim because he had a case of indigestion. He'd fired movie studio executives because he and Blythe were having an argument. I'd heard he'd once thrown a globe at an architect's head for bringing up a clause in a contract.

I leaned on the curving stone wall and peered over.

"Where is it?" Fairfax knocked Embry on the side of the head.

Embry ducked back. "I don't know."

Fairfax stared down at Embry. I hadn't realized until now quite how much height the father had on the son. "That swan was pure alabaster. Do you have any idea how much it's worth?"

A current shifted in me.

"Do you know how rare they are? I just acquired the match. I planned to show them to my guests as a complete set. But you didn't even think of that, did you?" Fairfax struck him again, the heel of his hand knocking into Embry's ear. "You choose poorly even when you steal, don't you?"

The alabaster swan. The one I'd taken and pawned to cover my car fare up and down this hill.

"Where is it?" Fairfax yelled down at him.

Embry started coughing, and when he said, "I don't have it," it sounded as though he had to wring the words from his body.

"What did you do with it?" Fairfax was yelling, but the music from the terraces veiled it from anyone at the party.

Embry was buckling in on himself, trying to shield his head. "I didn't" was all he managed to cough out.

The last strike landed, backhanded, on Embry's temple. He reeled back against the wall, and I couldn't see him anymore.

"I won't tolerate liars and thieves," Fairfax said, his voice level now. "You should know that better than anyone."

Fairfax strode out of the gardens.

I looked down for any sign of Embry. But he must have still been pressed against the wall. All I heard was him coughing. All I saw was his hands.

A few seconds later, wet leaves filled his palms.

He was pulling a thin garland out of his own throat.

The cord holding those leaves together looked so much like the vines on my body that my stomach turned over.

It wasn't just me.

Fairfax made his entrance into the party. As soon as he crossed onto the white marble of the poolside terrace, his demeanor changed. He was again the magnanimous host.

I stayed where I was for a long time, long after Embry left. I stood watching the party from a distance, my rage brighter than all the twinkling lights and all the globe lamps.

But this time, that rage didn't scare me. This time, it was as smooth as the rush of salt water from a wave. Instead of pulling at me, it took me in completely. Instead of it dragging me like a riptide, it made me part of its current.

There was something new about my anger now, something pure and distilled. I had hated Embry Fairfax because he was a Fairfax, but now, after what I'd seen, I felt an odd kinship with him. He had something in common with my brother, and something in common with me, and something in common with everyone Bixby Fairfax had ever tried to stamp out under his heel. It let me focus my rage where it belonged, like beams of light converging.

I could feel leaves twisting out of the vines on my legs. I could feel the wooden knobs of my spine bristling with growth and the possibility of new branches. When I breathed, the trees here all breathed with me. When I moved, their branches rustled and their canopies shrugged. Every tree here was part of my body. Every branch and vine was my hands.

I was like the sea nymphs, transforming themselves into flames, water, lionesses, serpents. Whatever trick I had to use, whatever form I had to take, I would do it.

Like they were my own hands, the low-hanging laurel branches wrapped around a marble pillar, one Bixby Fairfax would pass in just a few moments.

But once I started it, it kept going. The laurel branches didn't stop with that one pillar. They wrapped around more of them, one on each side of the first, and then two more, and two more. They cracked the white marble like chalk. They toppled the globe lamps from their perches, and a half dozen moons crashed to the ground and shattered. Crumbling marble rained down as the guests screamed and ran.

When Lisandro and I were little, Papá used to read us a story about a nymph who transformed her lovers into fish. Then one day, she accidentally turned herself into a fish, too. The image of all those dignified suitors growing tails and fins had kept us laughing, but Papá had wanted us to learn something. He'd wanted us to learn how easily your own tricks could turn against you.

Maybe I had never really understood until this moment. Not because of the destruction I was watching on the terrace. But because the bar where Hayden had been serving drinks was now beneath a rubble of white marble.

LISANDRO

DAMAGE CONTROL. THAT was why I was here again, behind Embry Fairfax's mirror. I needed to convince him that the ghostly girl had been a figment of everyone's imagination. She was the product of some rumor, a story that had swept through the guests so effectively they'd begun to see things. It was cleaner that way. Less chance for anyone to note similarities between her and me, and similarities between her and the Magnificent Karina who stood before them.

But I was hesitating. Every lie I told Embry was more bitter on my tongue than the one before. This boy thought I was made of light and energy, but I was made of teeth and broken glass. I was the searing cold of dry ice.

I moved the panel aside just enough to look through.

Embry wasn't drawing on pieces of cigarette cardboard. He was pacing, hands in his pockets. He was looking down at the whirling pattern on the carpet.

If I hesitated, I'd fail Lola, and I'd fail myself. If I wanted him, if I gave any room to wanting him, I'd lose my chance at getting somewhere I could be who I was.

Embry and I were nothing but a dead end. I had to leave The Coterie with him still thinking I was nothing but an apparition.

As he turned, a shadow lifted off his face. The light showed a bruise blurring across his temple. The dark blue of it stood in such contrast to the gold saturating the room, like a nebula in the middle of the sky during the day.

I set the lights. The next time his back was turned, I eased the panel out of place.

When he turned and saw me, he tilted his head down. The times before this, he'd looked either pleased to see me or like he'd been expecting me. Now he looked startled, caught.

"What happened?" I asked.

Embry shook his head. "It's nothing."

All the poison in me, all the sharp edges, spun down into something solid, like the metal at the center of the earth. I wanted to protect him and I wanted to avenge him. I wanted to fight whoever had given him that bruise. I was watching Alcyoneus being crowned with garlands that marked him for death, and I wanted to do everything Eurybarus had done. I wanted to take the garlands off his head and face the monster myself.

Embry wouldn't meet my eyes. "I can't believe you're even talking to me."

There was no glint of life in him, none of that faith and curiosity that made the air around him shimmer.

"I can't believe you ever even spoke to me," Embry said. "And I can't believe you ever helped me. You must hate me."

"Why would I hate you?" I asked.

"Because of my father," he said. "Because of everything he's done."

Bixby Fairfax had done plenty. The reels his movie studios had produced had ruined politicians who would have raised his taxes. The information broadcast through the newspapers and radio stations he owned had spurred on wars. His resort was stuffed with artifacts he'd stripped from around the globe, pieces of history he'd plucked as though turning through a catalog. To him, every church was a storefront. Every sacred monument was his boutique of curiosities. Every ancient site was his quarry.

"The things he's done," I said, "the things he's stolen, the lies he's told, none of that's yours."

"But it's worse than that, and you know it," Embry said.

His head was still tilted down, his expression shadowed.

"You're dead because of him," Embry said.

I kept quiet. But inside I was scrambling, trying to figure out what I'd said that had made him fill in my story this way.

"Bernal." Embry met my eyes. "That's your last name. Right?"

All those thoughts stilled, like a hand had clamped down over a bell.

"How did you know that?" I asked.

"You told me your name," Embry said. "Ovidio."

I had told him my father's name. And that mistake was now haunting me.

"That was enough for me to find your last name," Embry said. "Find out what happened to you. Why you're here, still. You died because of my father."

Even with how little I understood, I knew I didn't want him to go on.

"My father has never known how to wait for anything.

Including his precious mansion." Embry's jaw tightened. "Not even during an influenza outbreak."

Somewhere in my brain, a door was creaking open on rusted hinges.

"My father should have stopped construction," Embry said. "The architects told him to. Everyone told him to. But he refused. And from what I've heard, he made it clear that anyone who wanted to keep their jobs needed to stay. So it spread. And the workers got the worst of it."

Now that Embry had opened that door in my brain, I couldn't get it shut again. I was checking the timeline even though I didn't want to.

Our mother and father often had to go away for work, sometimes for weeks at a time. But they'd never told us they'd worked here.

The doors kept unlatching in my brain, and with each one, it seemed not only possible but logical. Our father had worked as a plasterer. The slashes of white on his clothes could have matched the outside of this building. Our mother often worked as a cook; she could have been part of the staff keeping the crews fed.

"I didn't die from influenza," I said. I was arguing with him about my father's death like it was my death.

"I know you didn't," he said. "At least not directly. Not right away. And when it happened, it was long enough after you left here that it must have seemed like it came out of nowhere."

The timing was matching up. The door was warping enough that I couldn't force it back inside the frame.

"You couldn't sleep at night, right?" Embry said. "You started sleeping during the day. You started walking around like you were inside a nightmare even when you were awake."

I couldn't stop it. I could see them now. How they looked as blank and vacant as statues, staring into nothing. I remembered the heat of their fevers under my palms, how they winced against their headaches. The muscles in my father's neck went tight as ropes ready to snap. I broke my mother's falls each time she tried to cross the room and her body crumbled underneath her.

"It's a form of sleeping sickness," Embry said.

A hinge broke.

The door flew all the way open.

Sleeping sickness.

The words matched up with the doctor's words from years ago.

The words twisted the past and the future together. My body became my father's body. My bones became my mother's bones. The ache and weakness in my muscles, the desperation for sleep, it was mine, and it was theirs.

Sleeping sickness, the doctor had told us. *Not the insect-borne sort. This is a different kind. One we're seeing more of this year.* He'd confirmed the match of their symptoms. He'd ticked off each on his fingers as though relating a story. But he spoke with the frankness of a man who knew my sister and I might be on our own soon. He knew he owed us the courtesy of speaking to us as adults.

"It comes in the wake of influenza," Embry said now. "Often after the sick seem to have recovered. It happened to a lot of people that year. So when the heavy rain came and the building season was over, my father got to pretend that everything was fine, even though people went home to their families and died."

Anger was pressing up from under his words.

"That's what happened to you," he said. "Isn't it?"

I was caught inside the memory of my parents' faces as they grew worse. My father's eyes darted at nothing. My mother screamed at nothing.

Then stillness. Sleep kept them under. The living statues that looked like our parents left us.

"That's why you're still here," Embry said. "Because my father's responsible for your death."

The matter of me was coming apart. Hate was the only gravity holding me together. Bixby Fairfax wasn't in front of me, but his son was, so I hated Embry Fairfax.

"I want to help you however I can," Embry said. "If holding my father accountable is going to help you, I'll make it happen. If making sure everyone knows what he did will help you leave here, I'll do it. Just tell me what you want me to do and I will."

I didn't care. I hated him for having blood that came from the man who killed my mother and father.

Their fevers and blurred vision. Their blank looks and slow or nonexistent reactions to noises and changes in light. How they slept during the day and wandered the house at night.

Our own parents became ghosts to us before they died. We'd been watching them die without even knowing it.

A blunt crashing noise rattled the building. It was so loud it sounded like someone had toppled a statue or a fountain. It rumbled on like an earthquake.

Embry startled toward it.

The moment he did, I vanished.

I made myself nothing but a shadow to Embry Fairfax.

LOLA

I FLEW DOWN the staircase and through the shadowed gardens, and I swore I could hear the laurel trees laughing. I could hear the warning voices of all the girls who'd ever thought they could win against men who declared themselves gods. I could hear every Daphne, every sister of Diopatre, cackling at how I'd thought I could outrun their same fate.

Sure, you might save yourself, they whispered. *But what will you lose for it?*

Members of the staff were trying to calm and guide the guests toward the house, but none of them wanted to go.

They all wanted to watch the latest spectacle, Blythe yelling at Fairfax.

"I told you!" She pointed an accusing finger at him, her gloves shining like meringue. "I've told you something was wrong with this horrible place since the beginning!"

Fairfax didn't yell back. He hardly seemed to register her

words. He looked more disbelieving, heartbroken, at seeing the pillars toppled.

I froze at the edge of the terrace, struck still by the sight of all that cracked marble. Broken glass glittered like ice under the pieces. The green of absinthe and the red of cherry syrup seeped out from underneath all that white.

"We never should have come here!" Blythe's yelling seemed to both startle and enrapture the guests. "You always said you were building this place for me, but it was never for me! I never wanted it!"

I wanted to scream with her or over her. Did anyone even keep track of Hayden or anyone else who worked here? Why were the women laying their hands flat on their bead-adorned dresses in relief? Why did the men all have that air of *thank goodness no one was hurt*?

"Hey."

The second I heard the echo of Hayden's voice, I turned around.

The seam between the gardens and the terraces showed him as an apparition. We each existed at the edge of a different world. While I stood on white marble, Hayden appeared above the flagstones stitched together with grasses and moss. I was the living being, and he was the spirit emerging from the green of the trees and the gold of the garden lanterns. The fit of his trousers and shirt, the way he'd arranged his hair, it was all how I'd seen him out in the hills last night.

I was imagining Hayden alive. I was seeing what I wanted to see, like every mark Lisandro and I had ever fooled.

"What's wrong?" Hayden asked.

The echo came off his voice. His voice sounded less like

the ring around a note and more like I knew it, the texture like tarnished brass. It sounded real, like he was truly in front of me.

I touched him as fast as I could. I wanted to know, as fast as I could, if he was alive and standing here.

"Wait," Hayden said. "Did you think—"

Before he finished the question, I kissed him, breathing in the smell of metal and citrus on his clothes. I kissed him, and he put his arms around me and kissed me back with all the brazen certainty of a boy. He kissed me back harder, and I became a girl made of violet flowers, and he became the one person at The Coterie I didn't know how to con anymore.

LISANDRO

I THREW MY suitcase onto my bed.

I opened every one of the Magnificent Karina's trunks.

The Coterie was death. It had taken our father and mother and who knew how many other fathers and mothers and brothers and sisters.

And if Lola found out before I could get her out of here, she'd lunge at Fairfax's throat with a shrimp fork.

Lola walked in on my packing flurry. "What are you doing?"

"We're leaving," I said.

"No"—she laughed—"we're not."

"Lola." My patience was already fraying. "Trust me. We have to go. I promise I'll explain later."

She planted herself in a tufted armchair.

"For the love of . . . ," I muttered under my breath.

"I'm not going anywhere until you tell me why."

I hesitated.

"If I tell you," I said, "you promise you won't do anything about it?"

"No," she said. "Tell me anyway."

"You promise you won't do anything illegal about it?"

"No," she said. "Tell me anyway."

"Fine," I said. "Then promise you won't try to murder anyone over it?"

"I'm nothing if not willing to compromise," she said. "Deal."

So I told her what Embry had told me.

She blinked a few times.

That was it.

Maybe she wasn't following how Embry had described our parents' deaths while thinking he was describing mine.

Or maybe she was going to tell me I was wrong, that the timing didn't match, that it couldn't. Maybe she could keep the doors in her brain shut better than I could.

Or maybe the truth had landed so heavily on her that she couldn't take its weight.

I knew instantly I'd made a mistake. I should have found a way to get her off this hill before I told her. I should have made sure she had the space to cry and scream instead of having to stay in character long enough for us to leave.

"Hey." I came closer to my little sister. "Are you in there?"

She tilted her face up.

She was holding her eyes wide not as though she was shocked, but the way she did when she was acting.

This wasn't the look of taking something in.

This was the look of her trying to produce a reaction.

"You knew." I'd meant it as a question, but in the space of saying it, any doubt evaporated.

She blinked slowly, as close to an admission as I'd get.

I stepped back. "How long have you known?"

"I've been doing research trying to dig everything up for a while," she said. "But I didn't figure it out for sure until a few months ago."

"A few months?" I laughed at the stupidity of my past self. "So your long afternoons at the library? Your urgent need to study classic acting instructional texts?"

"I was doing that," Lola said. "I was just also doing other things."

"Like what?" Anger seeped into my voice.

"Records," she said. "Articles. Reports from the few papers Fairfax couldn't control or bribe. News he tried to make sure got buried."

"Yeah, and what else were you doing? Coming up here, right? Haunting the daylights out of this place?"

As I said it, understanding broke over me. But instead of illuminating everything, it was like stirring up the bottom of a pond. Through the murk, I couldn't tell which shapes were living things and which were shadows.

"How could you keep this from me?" I asked.

"Would you have agreed to it if I hadn't?"

"Of course not," I said. "And not because I would have wanted to spoil your fun or get in your way or whatever it is you think I do. But because maybe I wouldn't have wanted to be around these people if I'd known. I wouldn't have wanted either of us to get within a mile of this place."

I put my fingers to my temples, as though I could reach into my own brain and sort everything out.

"Why wouldn't they tell us they worked here?" I asked.

"Why do you think? Look out there." Lola gestured to the window. Turrets from other wings of the building cut into the sky. "If this was the only job they could get, do you think they'd have been proud to tell us? A mansion for someone who thinks the world is a giant flea market set up just for him?"

Every wall in this room loomed over me. Every curtain and painting and decorative bowl crowded closer. I could almost hear the rustling of the paper and string hanging off each one, declaring its price.

It had all been worth more to Fairfax than the lives of those who'd constructed these walls.

"And you wanted us to come here why?" I asked. "Just so you could hate Fairfax in person? Take his money? Did you really think that was going to make you feel better?"

"Yes." Her voice sharpened. "Because the rage was eating me alive. Because the rage was becoming all there was of me. I needed to even the score a little, even though I know the score can never be even. I had to do something before all that rage swallowed what was left of me."

Quiet fell between us. Quiet, not silence. This was quiet so clear it had a ringing sound around it.

"I had a plan," Lola said. "For both of us."

"That you didn't tell me."

"Because you would never go along with it."

"And why do you think that is?" I asked.

"I had the steps all laid out," she said. "We were never going to solve the haunting. We were going to make it worse and worse until it drove Fairfax and Blythe away and this place had such a frightening reputation that none of the guests would ever want to come back. We were going to poison it for everyone. I didn't know exactly how we were going to do that part, but I knew we'd find a way. And then when you suggested I be the Magnificent Karina, it was perfect.

Everything fell into place. She would be the one to fail at solving the haunting, not us. It would be her reputation that took the damage, not ours."

"You let me think I was talking you into something you wanted the whole time," I said.

"No." Lola sat up straighter, as though this was the important part, the one place she had to object. "That really was your idea. I would've never thought I could impersonate her. I meant it when I told you I wanted to rip her hair out, because she was going to ruin everything, my whole plan. But when you suggested I play her, it was brilliant. Because if even the Magnificent Karina couldn't fix a haunting, if it was getting worse and she couldn't do anything about it, that would mean there's really no hope, right? And by then we'd still have enough money out of them to get everything we both wanted. It was a perfect plan. They all think they want special appearances from you now, but then just as they think I have the haunting under control, just as they think you're nothing but a curiosity, a sideshow, you're going to get menacing. Threatening. The ghost's going to turn on them."

"So you used me." I clapped slowly. "Well done. I thought you were my acting coach, but you were a sculptor. You were shaping me into the prop you and your little plan needed me to be."

Lola looked away.

"You wanted someone to frighten them? Well, guess what?" I opened my hands at my sides. "You cast me perfectly. You were working with a great raw material, weren't you? I'm a brown guy. I'm frightening enough to them as a living human being."

The silence thickened in the air.

"I'm sorry," Lola said softly. She almost sounded like she meant it. "But"—there it was, *I'm sorry, but*—"I'm not leaving now. We have a chance to take this place apart."

"Haven't you noticed?" I asked. "It's taking itself apart. It's falling apart, and it could fall apart on either of us."

"We can be careful," Lola said, her voice even softer. "You taught me to be careful. We can do this."

"Staying is a thousand miles from careful," I said. "And for what? Revenge?"

"Yes. Because what we lost, it has to count for something. It can't just get forgotten. It has to matter to someone other than us." A new electricity crackled through Lola. "Men like Fairfax, they take without even looking who they're taking from. They still talk about manifest destiny." She crammed centuries' worth of scorn into those two words. "Their version of destiny is to destroy people like us and our antepasados. They talk about it like it's a blessing from God, but I don't see them leaving room for God anywhere. Not unless you count the choir stalls Fairfax imported because he thought they added a certain je ne sais quoi to the dining room. They all talk about manifesting what they want. They think they manifest it all because it's their destiny. But they want to manifest us right out of existence. Their destiny is our disappearance."

Lola was getting at me in a way that only a sister could. She was reaching her fingers into my chest. She was picking a lock inside me that I'd kept closed so long it had rusted shut.

"You feel it, too," she said. "I know you do. I can see it. You can pretend that it's all me, but you and I both know it's not."

"Oh yeah?" I asked. "If you and I are so alike, how come you got to be the one to engineer all of this and I got to be your puppet?"

"Because you gave up!"

It sounded less like she was yelling and more like words she had held back were breaking out of her.

"You gave up." She reeled herself back in. "You've wanted us to get somewhere else for years, but you got stuck into thinking all we could ever do was get by. You thought the best you deserved was trying not to get the shit kicked out of you by people who hate you. But when you got the idea about the job here, I saw life in you that I hadn't seen in a long time. You had hope. You saw our chance at something better. You saw *your* chance at something better, and you were willing to go after it. I loved seeing that in you."

"Well, I don't know why you even needed me." I kept packing, as though sheer momentum might convince Lola. I hated my sister right now, but hell if I wasn't going to save her from this place anyway. Her plan was done. Our plans were done.

"Because if you did this," I said, "if you did all of this, if you're so much smarter than I am that it wasn't even worth telling me what happened to our parents, then I don't know what good I possibly was to you. Except to scare the gringos who can't think of anything more terrifying than a brown guy who can walk into any room of their house."

As I reached up onto a high shelf, Lola called out, "Wait, don't!"

My hands pulled down clothes I'd never seen. Trousers in unfamiliar fabrics. Neckties in bright burnout patterns. Shirts with expensive cuff links still on the cuffs.

I actually had seen these. On The Coterie's guests.

"Where did these come from?" I asked, my back still to Lola.

"The wardrobes of guests you'd despise just as much as I do if you got to know them," Lola said.

I turned toward her. "Do you know what happens if we get caught stealing?"

"Who said anything about getting caught?" she asked.

"And what was the point of this? Seeing what you could get away with? Petty vengeance? Your grand vengeance plans weren't enough?" I threw down the clothes. "I am so tired of cleaning up your messes."

Lola's eyes flashed back to me. "And I am so tired of being the one who has to care about everything. You want me to stay out of things. You want me to decide that things are none of my business. But people like Fairfax win because enough people decide that what he's doing is none of their business. People like him always want people like us to mind our own business."

She was on her feet now. "You're tired of cleaning up my messes? Human beings make messes. And I am so tired of being the only one of us who's an actual living, breathing, feeling human being. I am so tired of having to be the beating heart for the both of us."

She landed that hit deep enough that I stood there, stunned into stillness, as my sister walked out the door.

LOLA

I HAD COME here for revenge. I had come here to get back the smallest fraction of what had been taken from us. And I had gotten so close I could feel its weight in my hands.

But The Coterie was winning, just as it had years ago. It had taken our mother and father, and now it was blowing apart my brother and me.

Lisandro had looked at me as though I was something horrifying. It was a look I would have relished from anyone else. But from my brother, it was proof of everything I'd gotten wrong.

I went outside hoping the cold air would wake me up, sharpen me into knowing exactly what to do, give me the precise words that would make my brother not hate me.

Instead, I was sleepwalking.

The party was now completely different than the one I'd left. The café tables, the strings of lights, the metal canisters full of tulips had all been removed. The women had rearranged their hair into soft twists framing their faces, like paintings of the Muses. Both men and women wore flowing garb worthy of sculpted friezes. High heels and shined shoes had been replaced with ornate versions of ancient sandals. The young ladies looked like statues ready to hold urns and pour water into the fountains.

Instead of ending the party, the broken columns had inspired an antiquities theme. Fairfax was even wearing a laurel crown like Caesar Augustus.

Whatever happened here, Fairfax would transform it so that it looked like it had been their plan all along.

As I wove through the party, voices followed me.

"It was just wonderful," a starlet whispered about Lisandro's appearance; he had materialized in front of her and two of her friends. "The girls back home are pea green with envy."

"Well done," Fairfax said discreetly as I went by. "The sap is still white as a sheet. It was marvelous." He raised a glass to me and then turned to greet a guest.

"May I have a word?" A man raised a finger in the air, trying to summon me.

"Can you bring him back again?" a socialite crowded in to ask me. "Yvette was too scared to come last time, but she's plucked up the courage."

"Is he free tomorrow just after midnight?" another asked.

They pressed in with their champagne and scotch breath, their Rome-is-burning merriment, their efforts to push money into my hands even as I couldn't seem to uncurl my fingers to accept it.

I was ready to disappear. I was ready to turn into a thousand laurel leaves before I could make another mistake.

The crush of people breathed and moved around the marble terraces. The first way out I found was at the edge of the enormous pool. I kicked off my incongruous shoes and cast aside my wrongly themed hat. I threw off my out-of-place coat, revealing the raspberry tulle of my outmoded dress. I took the first step down into the water, and the glowing aqua swirled around my ankles. I took the next step down, and it flowed through my skirt. A few more steps, and I drifted forward, letting the water swallow me.

My dress billowed around me, and with the shimmer of air bubbles stirring the water, I looked like the Clover Clubs Hayden mixed up for the ladies. White foam on top of glowing pink. I was as insubstantial as a sugary cocktail. I'd made myself easy to consume.

When I was far enough underwater that I couldn't hear the rest of the world, I grabbed at my ankles, trying to rip the vines from my body. But they were so much part of my skin I couldn't even get my fingers around them. I couldn't even get a good enough grip on myself to rip myself apart.

I screamed so I wouldn't hear the laurel trees laughing. I screamed instead of saying the words spilling out of my heart. *You won. You've broken us. You've broken our family apart again.*

I was ready for my bones to be wood and my fingers to be leaves. I was ready to become a fir tree like Elate. Her brothers had waged war against the heavens, and she had mourned them so deeply that she transformed into boughs, growing as many needles as she'd cried tears.

But my brother hadn't waged war on the heavens. He would never be so foolish. My brother had been wounded in a war I'd started behind his back.

I screamed, waiting for a tree to twist out of my spine. I screamed, waiting to dissolve into a cloud of laurel leaves the guests could toss like flowers.

The shadows around me shifted. The light from the underwater lamps dimmed. The marble underneath me was cracking, like the floor of the ocean wrenching open. Tree trunks broke through, widening the ruptures. They spiraled up, growing boughs and branches. They grew through the water and toward me, rushing up like a kelp forest.

As the trees rose past me, the bark of their trunks roughened. Knots formed like gathered points in fabric. In the center of one of those knots, a curve of glass shone like a marble. Then another just like it glimmered from another tree knot. Every direction I turned, I found more. Constellations of reflective marbles flickered across the tree trunks.

Through the blur of the water, I could just barely see hints of color. Amber set within white like a flame inside snow. Rich brown against white like new growth breaking through frost. Pale blues and greens within white like oceans and islands under veils of clouds.

Eyes. From every knot in every trunk, eyes were blinking at me. They'd come up from the floor of the earth. They were every tree from every story our parents had ever read us. They whispered from their leaves and the pages of those books.

They were protective sisters transformed into poplars. *Did you learn nothing from our story?* they murmured.

They were heartbroken girls becoming sycamores, asking, *Didn't you pay attention to how vain the gods are, how vengeful they are toward any who threaten their vanity?*

They were swift-footed girls punished for their speed, transformed into olive trees, rooted to the ground. *Did you think men who consider themselves gods would be any different?* they whispered.

I rushed up for air and to get away from those eyes. When

I broke through the surface, a canopy of branches surrounded me. I treaded water, and the eddies around the trunks turned my skirt into a cloud of ripped tulle.

The trees had grown so tall and thickly leafed that I couldn't see the guests, or the turrets, or the broken pillars. It was all boughs and branches. It was all leaves falling toward the surface.

A shift in the currents made me turn.

Hayden was treading water alongside me, looking at me as though his curiosity and scrutiny was finally pinning something down.

He was finally seeing me for what I was.

LISANDRO

I'D ONLY EVER been conned one time. At least as far as I knew. The most talented con artists leave you never knowing they've had their hand in your pocket.

But that one time had cost us everything.

I was fourteen. Lola was thirteen. And there was a woman at a carnival who styled herself like a rich grandmother. Curled white hair, thick eyeliner, pancake makeup, too-bright lipstick. When I thought back on it, I was pretty sure that was all to make her seem wiser and less threatening. When I thought back, I couldn't remember any lines on her face, no wrinkles creasing her makeup from underneath. She couldn't have been older than forty, turning herself into a kindly old woman for the sake of her act.

I would've seen through that now. But back then, anyone over twenty was part of the amorphous mass of adults, so I wasn't looking closely enough to tell forty from the sixty or seventy she was portraying.

That was a good lesson in lying. Once you let go of your vanity, you were halfway there.

She had no apparent qualifications except a sign declaring her a conduit to the dead. We wouldn't have stopped if she hadn't stopped us.

"You," she said, as kindly as a witch in a candy house, "you both have such profoundly sad airs about you." And we were so hungry for someone to see the grief in us, to not have to explain it, that we were taken in.

How easy it was to con someone when you knew exactly what they wanted to hear.

How easy it was to know what they wanted to hear when it showed so plainly on their faces.

"Who you've lost has never left you," she said, "so much so that I believe you could speak with them again now."

She had already gotten us to stop walking. She had persuaded us to pause in the dizzy, intersecting orbits of the carnival. That was half the work. Getting the marks' interest. Getting them to step closer to an environment you controlled.

"Their love for you transcends time and space," she said. "And they're giving me the strong sense that there's something they want me to tell you."

Now I would have flagged her techniques from a mile away.

The compliments about our beautifully profound bond with the deceased. An easy assumption considering we were paying to hear from them.

The generic guesses. The woman hadn't known anything about how Mamá spiced her café de olla; she'd only wondered aloud if our mother used to make coffee for our father.

The equivocation. She didn't even really make guesses.

She simply asked if things might be true, if she was hearing the spirits correctly, and then waited for Lola to confirm or for my expression to show how wrong she was.

But I didn't recognize any of that back then. I didn't realize she was seeding hope into our chests, waiting for what she could harvest from us. She had made us the second we walked by. Of course we had lost someone. We were drifting through a carnival without smiling. Our clothes had been patched so many times that the darning was showing. Dulling stains had taken hold on the white of Lola's shirt because I chose to make sure she was fed over making sure we had soap, and sometimes by the time we could wash things, the stains had set.

At that moment, things had been better. We'd both gotten better at spotting what could turn into an odd job. The week before, I'd heard a businessman complaining about how the weather stripping in his rented house was squealing like a brass horn section on windy nights. I told him I knew how to fix it because I'd watched Papá do the same thing.

At that moment, we had enough money to breathe. We had soap. We had a room paid up for the week, with a proprietor who rented to a thirteen- and fourteen-year-old because he was either too drunk to look at us twice or too desperate to fill a vacancy.

I should have left the money in the room, even though the locks were so easily broken. I could have found a place to hide it.

I should have brought only enough to buy Lola a coated apple. Or two, because she could never decide between a caramel apple (the one she liked better) and a candied apple (the one she never liked to eat but that she admired like a shining red jewel).

I could have bought her an entire tray of each, and it would have cost less than the mistake I was about to make.

But Lola didn't want a coated apple.

She wanted this. I could see it in her desperately hopeful eyes as she looked up at me.

We had grown up on stories of hunters transforming into rivers. Royal scepters dripping with honey. Kings turning their own daughters into gold. Was it so impossible that Mamá and Papá might still speak to us?

So I paid the woman.

But once we were inside the small, striped tent, the medium realized how very special our situation was. What extraordinary individuals our parents must have been because of what extraordinarily elusive spirits they were. How very challenging it was proving to reach them.

Lola looked at me with such pleading hope that I couldn't say no.

I should have. I should have broken Lola's heart right then so that the woman at the carnival didn't shatter it like the candy shell on an apple.

But I had already paid.

So I paid more.

And we paid more again when the woman at the carnival told us that it was proving exceptionally difficult to reach the other side. That it was taking such indescribable effort. That there were such interfering forces, that we were in the middle of the worst solar storm since 1859.

I paid her more.

Every time she made an excuse, laced with pained sympathy, I paid her more.

That was something else I had yet to learn about confidence games. Every time you persuaded someone to give something up, it became easier to persuade them to give up something else and something else after that.

Before we knew it, she had every dime we'd been carrying. All we had were kind, vague words. Assurances that our mother and father loved us and that we would see them again. And, as she ushered us out of the tent, her invitation to come back soon, because we never knew what new messages might come through. That solar storm should let up any day.

I should have known better. Mamá and Papá had taught me better. Mamá didn't even trust a mirror without further inquiry. She taught us never to believe what we saw in the glass until we made sure the reflection was blinking at the same speed and frequency as we were, that it smiled when we smiled, that its eyes stayed the same color as ours. *Just because it looks like your face,* she told us, *doesn't mean it's you.*

Lola always remembered that one better than I did. She was the one who'd made us check every mirror in the Magnificent Karina's suite, just to be certain.

I should have let it go by now, everything with the woman at the carnival. But I could still remember what Lola sounded like crying that night, asking why Mamá and Papá were so far from us that even a medium with her own carnival tent couldn't reach them.

It wasn't until the next morning that Lola understood what had happened.

It wasn't until the next morning that the rage found her.

That woman inspired our act. She put the spite in us that

made us come up with it. We learned to do what was done to us, but we did it better. Cleaner. We did it in a way that meant we could look a priest in the eye on Sunday mornings. We swore we would never do what someone else had done to us.

It was our first and most unyielding rule: no grieving families. We never promised anyone rapport with those they'd lost. We never claimed to be able to reunite them, even briefly, with loved ones who'd gone to be with God. If they asked, we directed them to their surviving family members, their friends, their neighbors, their priests.

We made our own ghosts. We left the dead out of it.

And it had worked. With every performance, we'd made each other better. We made each other artists.

I'd only ever been conned once. Until now, when I'd been conned by my own sister. We were the grieving family, and I hadn't even seen it.

By the time I'd made any kind of order out of my own thoughts, Lola had gotten a head start on me.

I threw on my coat and messed up my hair. I prayed to God and every saint I hadn't yet offended that without the lighting and Lola's makeup, I looked nothing like the ghost I played.

I followed the stone staircases around the building. In the dark, the moon was a white round on the surface of the oil fountain.

A voice around the next bend made me pause.

"He must be in love," the voice said.

"Well, isn't that sweet?" A second voice was cloyed with sarcasm.

I drew back into shadow.

"Have you ever heard of anything more pathetic?" This

was the first voice, peppered with the laughter of both men. "Pining after a ghost?"

My understanding came laced with anger.

"He's not even man enough to interest another living homosexual?" one of them asked, laughter echoing off the stone.

"I guess even the queers won't get near him," said the other.

Maybe there were two of them. But I was Menestratus, ready to put on a breastplate of fishhooks and fight monsters.

After all, I was a boy who'd grown up defending myself from monsters exactly like this.

I came out of the dark.

I hit first.

I hit fast.

"What the hell—" Their words were clipped, offended.

Their confusion held no fear of ghosts or death. They had no idea I was the one haunting this place.

"Who the hell do you think you are?" one of them asked. Because they didn't know. They didn't know who or what I was or even if they'd ever seen me before. To them, brown boys all looked alike.

Embry had been right. I was a boy made of light. But I wasn't luminous or beautiful.

I was as deadly as lightning.

And I kept hitting until one of them got me in the ribs.

I fell forward. I grabbed for the fountain edge to steady myself but went down fast enough that my palms hit the oil. My hands shattered the moon. Oil soaked my sleeves and the front of my coat.

As I tried to get up, one of them shoved me back down, hard enough that oil splashed into my eyes and blurred my vision.

I couldn't even see where the next fist came from. As I turned, another struck the side of my face. Pain crackled through my jaw like wind blowing through embers.

It was my sister's voice in my head, my sister's blood in my body. For a second, I believed I could turn these men into beetles as vengeance for insulting boys like Embry and me. I believed Lola and I could turn them into frogs for filling their pools but never touching the water. We could transform them into ants for claiming they invented the plough. We could clip their words into the chatter of crows for thinking their voices were songs and ours were noise.

My anger grew edges. It grew spines.

My sister was right. Men like this wanted to manifest us out of existence.

But if they wanted to manifest me out of existence, they would know me first.

My sister and I had been raised on tales of nahuales drawing souls from their hosts' bodies. We grew up on stories of brujas who protected whole villages but needed the taste of blood in their mouths every month in order to do it. Whenever I had to go out at night, Papá made me hold a slice of onion in one hand and a penny in the other to repel vengeful spirits. Mamá always trimmed Lola's hair above her waist so that she wouldn't be easily fooled by moonlight.

These men had no idea who we really were.

No one here did.

The Coterie, my sister, and I shared one bloodstream, bitter and hot and poisonous. Our father had built this place the same way he and our mother had built Lola and me. Our blood lived in its walls.

I got up. I hit back. I went for their pretty faces and their hateful mouths. By the time they got me on the ground, their lips and temples were bleeding. Sure, Menestratus didn't survive taking Cleostratus's place, but he went down fighting. When the monster swallowed him, all those fishhooks killed the monster from inside.

I was on my hands and knees, trying to get up, failing. The oil I was still blinking out blurred everything. With each hit they landed, a current lit up my blood. My veins were filaments. I was made of nothing but light. I had no substance to me anymore, nothing to fight back with.

Just as they were pulling me up by my collar, another man appeared, and I knew I was finished. Two had gotten me on the ground. With a third, it was over.

He stood between me and the oil fountain, holding a flare of light.

The two men froze, still gripping me but not moving. We all watched the light filling his hands.

A match. The third man had struck a match.

As casually as if he'd just lit a cigarette, he tossed it at the fountain. The pool of oil burst into flames, illuminating the world enough to show me the third man's face.

The two men holding me dropped me. They scrambled away as the flowing ribbon of oil poured flames into the basin. They scattered as though they'd just been visited by an angel bearing fire.

I ran before the man with the match could get a good look at me. Because he knew my face better than anyone else here. And I needed him to think any resemblance was nothing but his imagination.

LOLA

OUR LIMBS STIRRED the water under the trees.

"You need to get away from me." I smiled just to show Hayden my teeth. "As fast as you can."

As Hayden moved, water filled his shirt and his vest. He breathed so slowly, and paused for so long, that leaves fell between us.

"Why?" he asked.

"Why?" My laugh cut through the air. "Look at all of this. Look at what happens to everything I touch. Bad things are the only things I do."

"Like what?" Hayden asked.

"I steal."

"That part I knew," Hayden said.

"I did it right with your clothes," I said. "But I've done it wrong before. I've done it really wrong. I did it so wrong someone got blamed for it." The image of Embry reeling back into that wall wouldn't leave me.

The betrayal on my brother's face followed right after it.

"And I hurt my brother," I said, my words unsteady as I treaded water.

"The priest?" Hayden asked.

My own lies wouldn't even get out of the way long enough for me to tell the truth.

"You know, when I was growing up," I said, "my mother and father read us a lot of different myths, and I was always trying to figure out what my favorite one was, and I never really did. But there's one I always loved that my mother told me, about the goddess of the dawn and the goddess of the moon. Do you know that one?"

"I don't think so," Hayden said.

"They were sisters," I said. "And one day the goddess of the dawn fell in love with a prince. And she managed to negotiate with the gods for his immortality. The trouble was she forgot to get eternal youth added into the bargain. So over all those immortal centuries, he aged and aged until he turned into a cicada, or a grasshopper, or a locust; it depends on who you ask."

The light glimmered off the water between us. Hayden was still looking at me, listening.

"So when the goddess of the moon fell in love with a shepherd, she wasn't about to make the same mistake," I said. "She negotiated not only for the shepherd's immortality but for his eternal youth. There was one catch, though: He'd be asleep forever. No laughing together, no scintillating conversations. Just a sleeping shepherd and the moonlight on his perpetually dreaming face. And in that story, the goddess of the moon was supposed to be so much smarter than her impulsive sister. But all she got to do was look at someone she loved who never even knew she was there."

The shadows of the trees wavered across the water.

"So every time I saw a cicada or a grasshopper or the moon, I thought, I'd never be that stupid," I said. "I'd never be as stupid as either of them. I was sure I'd think of everything, every possible catch. I was sure I was so smart. But the thing is that it's easy to be smart when it's someone else's story. When it's happening to you, when you're inside it, you're just as stupid as everyone else."

Hayden's face didn't twist into confusion or scorn. His expression was so open, so intent on what I'd say next, that for a second I could believe we were in some enchanted lake. I could imagine we were far from anyone who knew my name or any name I'd ever stolen.

"I meant what I said," I told him. "I don't take money from grieving families. But that's just about all I can say. If you knew everything, you wouldn't get near me."

Hayden's forearm cut through the water between us. His hand found my shoulder. "Try me."

And I almost did. I opened my mouth to tell him everything.

But then voices rushed in at the edges of the trees, and he looked as caught as I felt.

We swam to the steps. Hayden went up first, offering his hand to help me out. My skirt dragged behind me, soaked and heavy.

As soon as we emerged from the trees' shadows, everyone broke into applause. They were watching, marveling at the forest emerging from the water. They speculated about how it might have been done, as though all of this was the most wondrous magic trick they'd ever seen.

The Coterie had broken apart my family, and here I was, delighting its guests.

I put away the scream still inside me.

I let the performer I was take hold of my body.

In my line of work, you did whatever you needed to do in order to get away with what you had done.

In my dripping skirts, I curtsied like an actress after a play. I bent low, showing my gratitude that they should be so kind as to watch my little show. And the cold let them think I was shivering instead of trembling with how badly I wanted to rip apart all of them and all of myself.

LISANDRO

THERE'S A MUCH-UNDERRATED skill in my line of work: knowing when a job has gone irreparably wrong.

Lola always called it getting caught in a thunderstorm. *You know*, she'd say. *A sudden downpour. Lightning. And you're the tallest thing in an open field. Nothing to do but take cover.*

This more than qualified. Those men might not have recognized me, but Embry could have. He might have witnessed that I was solid, corporeal, very much alive. Even the most gullible mark couldn't be drawn back in after that.

Nothing to do but take cover.

The sooner I disappeared, the harder Embry would wonder if he'd really seen what he thought he saw, and the more of a chance Lola and I would have to get out of here. She could be mad at me for messing this up. I could be mad at her for what she'd kept from me. We could be mad at each other all we wanted. We just had to get out of here first.

That started with losing Embry.

I kept thinking I could hear his footsteps behind me. But with the noise of the party on the other side of the building, I couldn't tell for sure. And I couldn't stop to look back. So I'd play this safe. I'd make sure I outran him.

As I got to the edge of the manicured grounds, I threw off my coat and dropped it on a stone path. It was heavy with oil, slowing me down. And the sooner I ditched it, the less of a clue it would give Embry.

The brush-covered hillsides draped down like pooling gold fabric, buttoned with the green of live oaks. If I was lucky, maybe Embry was afraid of mountain lions or coyotes. Maybe he saw their reflective eyes in the hills as the lights of some strange, unknowable city and wouldn't go past the begonia borders.

As I got farther into the hills, oak branches scraped my arms. Olive leaves brushed over my skin. I prayed that with every tree I passed, I was making it harder for Embry to find me.

But every time I blinked, the darkness around me was different. Wispy leaves became enormous eyelashes. The pale bud blossoms on trees turned to teeth. The texture on bark bleached to the shine of fingernails.

Branches reached out with the force of hands, slowing me down. The boughs were arms holding me back. It all pressed in, the teeth, the fingernails, the screens of eyelashes, the blinking of watching eyes set in hollows of wood. The leaves closed in like hands over my eyes.

Back when he thought I was a ghost, when he thought we were separated not just by mirror glass but by death, Embry Fairfax had told me about vignetting. How images stretched and darkened at the corners because cameras and maps failed to reflect real life the closer you got to the edges.

This was how I was losing the world around me, losing my sense of which way I'd come. It started at the corners first, then the edges. Then the rest of it burned up and crumbled to ash. There was nothing in the universe but these trees closing in.

The fingers of a branch landed on my arm. I whirled around, ready to shove them off me.

Embry set his palms on my upper arms, stopping me.

His mouth was open, paused in the middle of whatever he could not manage to say. His eyes were wide enough to reflect the broken moonlight and the shine of the oil on my hair.

His grip tightened.

My solid, warm body under his hands was all the proof he needed of what he already knew.

"You got me," I said. It came out hard, bitter, shot through with a cruel laugh.

His arms pinned me in place. He was strong enough that I couldn't twist out of his hold as easily as I would've thought. He had me, all because I was stupid enough to fight those guys for what they were saying about him.

He stared at me, uncomprehending. He looked at me like he still wanted to reach across realms and touch me, the boy he thought was made of light. Even though he was holding me still. Even though he now knew I was a liar.

"Okay?" I said.

I wanted this over with. As long as none of this blew back on Lola, he could do whatever he wanted. I would figure a way out of this.

"So what are you gonna do?" I asked.

As long as none of this touched her, I wouldn't fight him.

"Just do it, okay?" I threw the words at him.

His expression sharpened, as though he was coming awake. He understood now. The wonder was gone. In its place was a slight smile, feral and proud. It was finally dawning on him that he'd won. He could revel in the pride of having caught me.

"Do what you want with me," I said.

His laugh was short, like he'd clipped off the end of it. "Yeah?" His tone was as confrontational as mine, and it was almost thrilling. I had dragged him down with me. I had gotten him down into the mud, and I would keep him here long enough for Lola to get away clean.

"Yeah," I said. "Do it."

As fast as a current through a circuit, Embry Fairfax moved his hands into my hair.

He kissed me in a way that could have turned blood into roses. When I opened my mouth to his, he kissed me hard enough to turn salt water into amber. He kissed me harder than I'd ever been kissed, and anything in the universe was possible. A spill of milk could become the trailing edge of a galaxy. A boy whose father I hated became someone who bent light around him. The dark, quiet star where my heart had once been pulsed and blazed back to life.

LOLA

MY DRESS TRAILED behind me, the damp tulle dragging on the hallway carpet as I walked. All I wanted was to sleep and to dream up the exact words that would make my brother forgive me.

When a tall man rounded the corner, it was his grandly draped costume I saw first. A golden pin winked at his shoulder. He looked as though he had just jumped down from a painting.

Bixby Fairfax was still in his emperor costume.

"Just who I wanted to see," he said.

For the love of the heavens, what did he want now? Did he have a room full of ladies who needed their fortunes read by how their mascara coated their eyelashes?

"Come." He gestured back around the corner. "There's someone I'd like you to meet."

He ushered me into a room paneled in wood as dark and ornate as the hallway. It was small, close, with a low ceiling and a desk whose carved legs looked as heavy as stone.

In an upholstered chair sat a woman, her milk-pale hands resting on the brocade arms. The satin of her dress was the exact shade of absinthe lit by a flaming sugar cube. No, brighter. The green a child would color in a field. The green of the croquet lawn in full sunlight. The green of the grass tennis courts at noon.

That green was now the color of my horror. Second only to the new-penny copper of her hair, the same shade I wore on my own head.

She was in profile, and I could see the shine of her red lipstick. The lamp cast a highlight on the glossy finish, like the wax on an apple. Against the white of her skin, the red was shocking, as if the queen on a playing card had come to life.

Margaret Drummond, the real fraud, the original Magnificent Karina, turned. And when her eyes found me, she smiled.

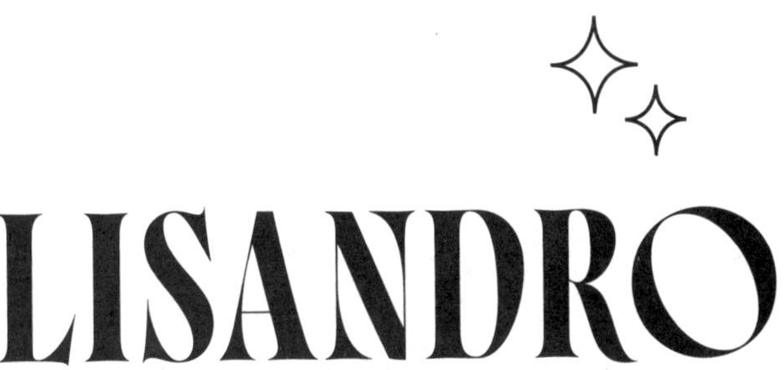

LISANDRO

"HERE." EMBRY WRAPPED a cloth around a piece of ice.

I held it to the side of my face. "Thanks." My voice sounded tight and dry, a fossil sealed in resin.

Now that the rush of fighting and then the rush of Embry kissing me was wearing off, pain crackled through me.

Embry poured water into a glass and handed it to me.

"You don't have to sit down there, you know," he said. "There's a chair. There's the bed." As soon as he said that last part, he blushed, the color in his face the same as the coral in his fingertips. "I mean you don't have to sit on the floor."

I drank half the water in one swallow. "It's a little disorienting being on this side of the mirror." I blinked against the headache surging from my temples and into my brain. "I guess being close to it feels like less of a stretch." I tapped the back of my knuckle against the mirror's frame.

I finished the glass, and the starburst of pressure in my forehead started to ease.

"What are the odds they recognized me?" I asked.

"The guys out there?" Embry sat on the floor next to me. "With how drunk they were? About the same as the odds they paint a passable forgery of a Rembrandt."

Embry reached for my hand, and all the stars outside seemed as close as spilled salt.

"You still look like you're ready to fight." He pried my fingers away from my palms.

"I never realize when I'm doing that." I tried to relax my hand, to let it fall into his, but my tendons felt taut and stiff. "My sister says I sleep with my hands balled into fists."

It took a second for me to catch my own slip. *My sister.*

"You're really not turning me in?" I asked.

"To who? My father?" Embry let go of my hand. "That's why you're here, isn't it?" He set his back against the wall next to me. "To settle the score with him, right?"

I stared into the room, trying to parse how much I was going to tell him. The only math that made sense was that I would lie just enough to keep Lola out of it. That was it. For everything else, I'd tell Embry the truth.

"Ovidio Bernal was my father." I shut my eyes. If there was any pity in Embry's expression, I didn't want to see it, not even in my peripheral vision. "My mother worked here, too."

"Shit," he said. "You lost them both?"

I nodded, eyes still closed.

"You and your sister lost them both," Embry said. Not a question.

I opened my eyes.

"Come on," he said. "How stupid do you think I am? Now that I'm getting a good look at you?"

A bolt tightened in my chest.

"That's your sister, right?" he asked.

I didn't confirm.

I didn't have to.

I let my head fall back against the wall. "You can do whatever you want with me."

"I did." There was a laugh in Embry's voice again. "I am."

I shoved his upper arm.

Then I looked right at him. "But you know if you try to turn her in, I'll kill you in your sleep, right?"

"I won't," he said.

He didn't seem as afraid as I wanted him to be.

"I'm not kidding," I said.

"I didn't think you were," he said. "I'm not telling anyone anything."

"Thank you," I said. "Just let us pack up and we'll be gone. I promise it'll be like we were never here."

"But what about"—Embry sounded like he was trying to catch the end of a question—"I thought"—but it was slipping from his grasp. "I don't want you to leave."

"Why not?" I asked. "I lied to you. And until tonight, as far as you knew, I wasn't alive. I wasn't even really there. I was never really here to you."

"Who says a ghost isn't really here any more than any of us?" he asked. "We're all mostly empty space, even when we're alive. We're mostly the distance between electrons, the same way galaxies are mostly the space between stars. We're as sparsely materialized as the night sky. Most of the universe and most of us are blank space. So if you think about it, the only difference between the living and the dead is that the living are dense enough to be felt by the living. Maybe if we paid attention, we'd feel the dead, too."

I shivered with the memory of every time I'd helped Lola

cut her hair above her waist, as though our mother was in the room. I could almost hear Mamá whispering that a few too many inches of braid left a girl gullible by moonlight.

"I was the one who didn't feel real," Embry said. "When we met, I hadn't felt real in a long time. But you were electricity in a dark room. Every time I talked to you, it was like I was collecting light."

It didn't make sense. I'd made Embry believe, and then I'd shown him the lie I was. Yet it hadn't shaken his faith in the magic of everything else.

"And then when I saw you"—Embry was smiling, shaking his head at the floor—"for a second, before I realized what you'd done, I thought maybe I'd managed to wish you to life."

We were both still, the same current jumping between us.

Once, Mamá told Lola and me about the electrical impulses in our hearts. She told us that when people talked about feeling a spark, they weren't talking about magic any more than they were talking about science. *It's something real,* she told us. *Remember that when it happens to you. You're not imagining it.*

But I needed to ignore this one. I needed to transform this spark into one I was imagining.

"There's nothing here," I said.

"Like hell there's not," he said. "I felt it. You felt it."

I got up from the floor. "It doesn't matter."

"Why not?" he asked.

"Because I don't want you to die."

I didn't realize I was raising my voice until I heard it echoing off the half-orange ceiling.

Embry got up, slowly, keeping eye contact the whole time. He folded and unfolded his limbs as efficiently as collapsing a card table. I hated how easily he added to the odd collection of things that made me want him.

"What are you talking about?" he asked.

"Every single story about boys like us." I set down the ice. "You know what happens. Boys like us don't live. We get destroyed. One of us or both of us. That's the story. That's always the story. That's what happens to us." The air was going out of me. The fight was going out of me. "We know how this ends."

Calamus and Carpus. Achilles and Patroclus. Apollo and Hyacinthus. These were the ghosts who followed me. Their histories cast shadows on every future I could ever have.

"Have you heard of first light?" Embry asked. "With telescopes?"

"What does that have to do with anything?" I asked.

Embry moved two pieces of cigarette cardboard to the middle of the desk. "First light is the first use of a newly constructed telescope." He took a pencil from his shirt pocket the way the guests here took out their silver lighters.

"Is that a golf pencil?" I asked. "Do you walk through life perpetually ready to keep score during a golf game?"

"No, I do not." He was trying not to smile. I could see the tension at the corners of his mouth.

"No, really," I said. "Are there a great number of surprise tournaments?"

"I don't play golf," he said. "Especially here. Arrogant guests who all want to show off, lobbing projectiles at lethal speeds? I'll pass, thank you. But I do appreciate the space efficiency of the writing implements." He sketched blurred shapes and crosshatches on one piece of cardboard. "With first light, that first image produced is rarely usable. It hardly shows anything clearly. But it's only by taking an imperfect first image that it's possible to learn what needs adjusting." He drew on the second piece of cardboard, this time in cleaner shapes, the points of stars, the forms of constellations, the spirals of galaxies. "You don't get the image you can see clearly without the one that's blurry."

He set the pencil down and looked at me. "So you're right. That's the story. Boys like us die. That's what we hear over and over, if we hear anything at all. And the only way it will ever look different for us is if we look at it differently. The only way to see something clearly is to be willing to see it when it looks nothing like you think it should."

The dark filament of my heart was lighting up. I wanted to hide it from him before he saw it through my shirt.

"I don't want you to leave." For a few seconds, his look was so earnest, and then the smallest smile came to his lips. "At least not until you've taken this place for everything you can."

"And then what?" I asked.

"What do you mean?" he asked.

I had broken so many of my own rules. I was caught in a thunderstorm. I was a lightning rod. And I knew enough to know that falling in love made you stupid, but that wasn't stopping me.

"When we leave, why don't you come with us?" I took the ice and put it against the older bruise on his face, where it was turning yellow and greenish. "We don't know exactly where we're going, but it'll be somewhere with a lot more people like you and me than there are here."

"You really need to take look at how some of the ladies hold each other's gloves," he whispered, as though gossiping at dinner.

"I mean it," I said. "Come with us."

For a second his smile was open, like all the possibilities were finding space inside him.

Then it collapsed.

"I wish I could." He took the ice off his face and put it back into my hands.

"So you'll just stay here?" I asked. "Why?"

He shrugged. "It's a little complicated."

"Really?" I asked. "You know everything you know about me, and all you tell me is 'It's a little complicated'?"

Embry turned away. He neatened the pieces of cigarette cardboard on the desk.

"Is it because of what happens to you?" I asked.

He froze.

"The leaves in your throat," I said. "Is that why it's complicated?"

His shoulders tensed.

"Look," he said, his back still to me. "I'll help you however I can. But you don't need to help me."

"Embry." I took a step closer. "Why are you still here?"

"Do you know how many questions I'm not asking you?" His voice sharpened. "Could you maybe do the same for me?"

A series of light knocks skipped on the door.

"Embry, darling!" Blythe's voice sang from the hall.

I was instantly alert, looking around for places to hide.

"Don't bother," Embry whispered, resting his forehead on the desk. "I'm not opening the door."

"Your father wants to see you," Blythe said. "And apparently I'm his messenger girl tonight." The cheer in her voice was varnish over a note of resentment.

"It's two in the morning," Embry said. "He hasn't poured himself into bed yet?"

Blythe laughed. "You're too much. I think he's in his study."

"Which one?" Embry asked.

But Blythe's shoes were already tapping down the hall.

Embry lifted his forehead off the desk and set it back down, over and over, pantomiming banging his head into the wood.

I put my hand between his forehead and the desk.

He landed on my palm and stayed there. "I'll be right back," he said, his eyes closed, his voice almost a groan.

Then he straightened up to look at me. "Stay here, okay?"

"I have to make sure my sister's all right," I said.

"And how are you going to do that without anyone seeing you?" Embry asked. "If the party's still going, she's there with everyone else. So I'll go demonstrate whatever filial piety my father insists on, and then I'll find her and bring her back here."

"She's not going to want to talk to you," I said. "I can promise you that."

"I'll tell her I have a ghostly problem in my room," Embry said. "If she thinks I don't know anything, she'll have to take it seriously to stay in character as a medium. Once she's up here, I'll let you explain everything." He reached for my hands and uncurled my fingers again. "I think I know how I can help you both."

LOLA

MARGARET DRUMMOND COOLLY accepted a cigarette and light from Fairfax. "She's a fraud, you know." She was talking to Fairfax, but she blew her first puff of smoke at me.

"You're the fraud." I stood in front of Fairfax's comically gigantic desk. "Do you know what she's done? The grief-stricken families she's bilked? She's an affront to my calling."

Margaret slowly rose from the chair, making a study of my face. "Look at that blush. What gutter did you fish yourself out of?"

My hands were ready to rip the beading from her dress.

But as fast as the impulse came, another followed it. I wouldn't do this again. I wouldn't handle her on my own this time. Lisandro and I doing this together was our only way out.

"I'm the true medium," I said. "I can prove it."

I was already formulating the test in my mind. It would be a spectacle. Two dueling mediums, each out to show that she was the true Magnificent Karina. Fairfax would love it. And I would come out the victor, because the ghost of The Coterie would appear only for me.

"Ladies." Fairfax patted the air. "Enough." He nodded to Margaret Drummond. "A car is waiting to bring you to your accommodations. A longer drive than we'd like, but I wouldn't dream of putting you in that flea-ridden excuse for a hotel they have in town here. I think you'll find the suite I booked you at Palais-aux-Cailles to your liking. It's one of their best. And the remainder of your payment will be wired by morning."

Payment? For what? She hadn't done anything.

"That's my dress you're blaspheming with your body." Margaret Drummond sauntered past me. "She's not just a fraud; she's a thief."

"I think that's enough," Fairfax said with the voice of a tolerant grandfather. "Thank you very much for coming." He shut the door behind her. "Now, let's have a little chat, shall we?" He smiled like I'd taken a good turn at croquet. "You, young lady, have had a secret partner in crime, haven't you?"

The damp tulle of my dress felt coated in ice.

"Someone working behind the scenes," he said. "Invisibly. Imperceptibly. Someone who helped you obtain this most advantageous opportunity to win more money than you ever dreamed of."

He was enjoying this. I would have felt less fear if he was screaming in my face.

"It's been very curious around here," he said. "Things have gone missing. Things have been stolen."

The red-and-gold sweep of Fairfax's costume made him look like an emperor on a Roman coin. I tried to imagine him like that, small enough to fit on a coin, small enough that I'd have nothing to be afraid of.

"And then the lady contacts me to say that her things have been stolen, along with her very name," Fairfax said. "Now, I wouldn't be a very good businessman if I didn't know how to put things together."

He wasn't a good businessman. His entire persona as a successful businessman was a joke, all dependent on draining his family's money.

"So I began to wonder, what might these things have in common?" Fairfax asked. "The pilfering of precious objects, the theft of a woman's persona. The thing they both have in common is a desire for money. Now, it wouldn't be any of my staff. I pay them well. And I look each of them in the eye before I hire them. I'd be able to spot a thief."

A knock came on the door.

Fairfax didn't turn his head.

"So I asked myself, who else?" he said. "Who around here do we already suspect might be a thief?" After a long pause he looked toward the door. "Come in."

Embry Fairfax entered the room.

The gravity left my body. My organs no longer felt anchored in place.

"Blythe said you wanted to see me?" Embry said.

"I thought I might see you two together." Fairfax stood back. "Observe the team side by side."

"Sir?" Embry sounded even more confused than I was.

Don't say anything. I wanted to shove my thoughts into Embry's head. *Don't say anything.*

"How did you work it out between you?" Fairfax's pointing

finger moved from Embry to me and back. "Did you agree to split it?"

Embry searched my face.

Don't talk. I would've jammed my thoughts into his ear if I had the chance. *Don't talk.*

"Treachery from a show-woman." Fairfax shook his head at me, almost pitying. "I would expect nothing less. But from my own son?" As he turned to Embry, all amusement left his face. "I expect loyalty."

"Loyalty?" Embry let out a breath of a laugh. "Like you were *loyal* to my mother?"

Fairfax backhanded him fast enough that I didn't see it coming. His hand flew out, and the side of Embry's face flushed red.

The sound of the impact lingered in the room.

Embry looked down, breathing hard, his hair falling in his face.

Don't say anything, don't say anything, don't say anything. The thought rang in my head as two men came in. Not members of the staff. Guests. Two of the men who always had caustic words on their tongues for boys like Embry. Boys like my brother.

"He had nothing to do with it," I said to Fairfax as the men moved toward Embry.

But Embry lifted his head, a sheen of defiance in his eyes.

"You hate me because I know." Embry stared right at his father. "Just like they knew."

With a sigh that fell somewhere between exasperation and disappointment, Fairfax looked down at his desk. "Every time I think you're through with these delusions."

Shut up, I wanted to scream at Embry. *Shut up before you make everything worse for yourself.*

But I recognized that look in his eyes. It was the glint of having nothing to lose.

"I know who you really are," Embry said, louder now, "just like they knew."

"Get him out of here." Fairfax waved a hand toward the door. The light flashed off the ring on his thumb.

The men each took hold of one of Embry's arms. Like Fairfax, they were still wearing their costumes from the party, expensively patterned fabric gathered into ancient-looking robes. It added to the strangeness. It made every awful thing seem possible. They could pummel Embry with their words and their fists. They could throw him off this hill, a mortal cast off their divine mountain. They could throw him into an ocean that would dissolve his bones.

"I know!" Embry was fighting their grip, shouting as they dragged him out of the room. "And you know I know! You can lie about it, but it still happened! Everything happened! It all still happened!"

As they pulled him down the hall, his words cut out, replaced by the sound of him coughing, like the air in his throat was turning to leaves.

"He didn't do anything," I told Fairfax again.

"Why such nobility?" Fairfax asked. "If he's won your heart, if he's made you think you've won his, then he's pulled one over on you, because I assure you, that's impossible. Ask anyone. So what was your plan?" The cold judgment he wielded toward his son fell away. His amusement returned. "Divert the Magnificent Karina, have you take her place, and then you'd share in the fee? I imagine the plan was yours, because it's inspired."

"Why would he steal?" I asked. "He's your son. He has everything he could want."

Fairfax looked touched, as though I'd understood the truest thing about him. "You would think that, wouldn't you? But he insists on sending money to his sisters. Awful, ungrateful girls. Be glad they're not here."

I listened toward the hall, waiting for the heavy footsteps of the men returning for me.

"I can explain," I said. "Everything."

Fairfax raised his hand.

I flinched.

Then I realized it was a gesture to stop me talking.

"Do you know why I paid the Magnificent Karina to keep quiet?" Fairfax asked. "Do you know why I reimbursed her so exorbitantly for her lost wardrobe? It wasn't some favor to you. It wasn't even a favor to Blythe, as much as she's taken to you. It's because your fraud is better than the original. Even the most impressive stories about her don't match what you can do. So as far as I was concerned, you deserved the name. And my guests deserve the best show there is."

Disgust roiled through my rib cage.

"I don't know how you do half of what you do," Fairfax said. "You're very talented. But you know what I respect even more than that? You did what you had to do. You took what you had to take. You were willing to do what so many others wouldn't have the stomach for. You were ruthless. You thought of no one but yourself, and you were smart about it. I would've been lucky to have a daughter like you."

My disgust coiled into a knot. It felt permanent, ancient, like sap hardening into amber.

"Now, get some sleep," Fairfax said. "And don't lose a wink over your partner in crime. The money's all yours now. He won't be asking for his half."

I turned toward the door. I watched my hand reach for the knob.

Mamá used to say that risk is a flower that blooms, and its season is whenever you're sure you've thought of everything. I'd thought my every crime was invisible. But each one had been a seed. I'd been scattering them behind me. Now they'd grown into brambles tearing at my skirt.

"And speaking of money," Fairfax said.

I stopped mid-step.

"That was quite the display tonight," Fairfax said. "The trees in the pool. I'll assume the trick's conclusion is restoring the marble to its original state. And if not, no need to worry. I'll simply deduct the cost of repair from your fee."

I turned the doorknob. I felt everything—the money Fairfax owed us, the plans Lisandro and I had made for it, the vengeance meant to quiet the rage in my heart—falling from my hands.

LISANDRO

AS I WAITED for Embry, I looked through the cigarette cardboard. There were as many pieces as there were playing cards in a deck. Some were sketches of circuits and filaments. Ideas for novel lamps and lighting fixtures. The elements of a camera obscura. A hundred perfect circles, overlapping like bubbles or like points of light seen through water.

As I shuffled through the cards, the optical sketches parted, revealing a new layer underneath. Drawings of gnarled boughs and twisting branches. Tree trunks with spiraling stripes of bark. Repeating patterns of leaves that covered the cardboard in dashes of silver pencil, like a close-up of foliage. And at the bottom of each one, in script as twisting as the branches, was a set of four words. On one, *We could be anything*. On another, *Anyone can be anything*. On another, *We could be anyone*.

Every card that had a fragment of a tree had one of those sentences.

We could be anything.

Anyone can be anything.

We could be anyone.

There was the breath of something sinister in those words. I could feel them whispered against the back of my neck.

Embry hadn't wanted me asking about the leaves that came from his throat. He had spoken so openly about everything else, even his father's crimes. But he wouldn't let me near that.

It started as a hitch of suspicion, something shifting out of place. And the longer Embry was gone, the more obvious it became.

Embry Fairfax had conned me.

He had gotten me to stay here, on this side of the mirror, so that he could bring back witnesses. I had been taken in by this boy who could draw leaves off his tongue as though they were words. I had learned nothing from the stories Mamá and Papá had told Lola and me. I was as foolish as Actaeon, looking at someone beautiful and dangerous. With a flick of his wrist, Embry had splashed water on me and transformed me into a stag, and now he would bring back the hounds who would tear me to pieces.

I'd been foolish enough to fall in love in the middle of a job. I'd been stupid enough to think Embry had been telling me the truth, when I had told him so many lies.

Lola's voice reverberated in my head.

Con artists make perfect marks because they think they can't be conned.

Lola. I'd been stupid enough to give Embry a head start to get to Lola.

I crossed the room, my body charged with how badly I had to get out of here, how badly I needed to know if Embry had thought of everything, including locking me in. If he'd tried, I'd break this door down. I'd splinter the antique inlay. I'd shatter the mirror glass and go through the wall. I had to find Lola, even if it meant everyone seeing me in broad daylight.

My hand had just reached the doorknob when a tapping sound came from behind me.

"Hey," a voice whispered.

The image of Lola appeared in the mirror.

It was all wrong. It was the world inside out. Lola was the ghost behind the mirror, and I was on this side of it. It was so wrong I wondered if she was dead. As I took in the image of her on the other side of the glass, my fears painted the whole scene for me. Embry or his hounds cornering her. Her fighting back, trying to scratch their eyes out, trying to escape. How it could have ended with her falling off a balcony or a staircase.

"Hey." Lola knocked her knuckles against her glass. "What are you doing in there?"

Her tone was so irritated that it pulled me back.

Lola disappeared out of the frame.

"Lola!" I whisper-yelled at the glass.

A minute later, she came through the door of Embry's room.

"What's going on?" I asked.

I hadn't even finished the last word before my sister threw her arms around me. Tight, like she hadn't in years.

I wrapped my arms around her, the kind of older-brother hug I barely remembered but that lived in my muscle memory.

I shut my eyes, wincing against what I had to tell her.

"Lola, I did something really bad," I said.

"So did I," she said into my shirt.

"It's okay. We'll figure everything out." I patted my hand against her hair. She was so much my little sister that it was jarring to find the red hair under my fingers. "We've just got to get out of here first."

"We can't." Lola pulled away. "We have to do something. They took him."

"Who?" I asked.

"Embry," she said. "They took him, and it's because of what I did."

"What do you mean?" I asked. "Took him where?"

"I don't know," Lola said. "But Fairfax thinks Embry helped drive the Magnificent Karina out of town so we could get this job."

Panic for Lola rose inside me, looming alongside my panic for Embry.

"Fairfax knows?" I asked.

"He knows." Lola's laugh was clipped and bitter. "He doesn't care as long as we're giving everyone a good show and making sure his precious resort stays the most coveted invitation there is. But he's coming down on Embry, and I don't know what he'll do with him."

I looked at my sister's face, pinched with worry for someone she had every reason to despise.

"We'll find him," I said.

"How?" she asked.

Under the red hair and the makeup that transformed her into the Magnificent Karina, I saw the girl I'd grown up with.

"You think you can get back into your creepy dead-girl character?" I asked.

The worry in her face softened, giving way to a wicked smile.

In the chilling ghost-girl voice that haunted my dreams, she said, "Always."

LOLA

FROM THE LOOK of the empty wine bottles, the men who'd taken Embry had celebrated a job well done. They were passed out on poolside furniture, their costumes rumpled, like a vignette from a morality painting. I could almost picture the scene done in tile work, Minerva above them, rolling her eyes at the dregs of a wild party at a magistrate's villa.

But there was no Minerva. There was only me, a girl made pale by makeup, my dark hair obscuring my face. I loomed on the edge of the terrace above them. The layers of my dress, white tinged with blue like ice, floated around me. Dyed-syrup blood dripped from my eyelashes, my mouth, my fingers. Luminous paint highlighted each trail of it, as though my blood was glowing poison.

With a sound between a gasp and a scream, I woke them.

Their eyes were hazy from drinking as they blinked up at me.

"Where has he gone?" I spoke down to them.

Fear sobered them up fast, jarring them awake.

"The son of the man who built this pretty palace," I said, my voice going higher. I sounded both sweet and deadly. I was the little ghost girl who wouldn't hesitate to rip the head off a doll or a living man. "Where is he?" I stretched my arms out, and the ribbons trailing off my sleeves added to the illusion of me floating above them. "I have a quarrel with his soul."

The men gripped each other's arms, as though trying to wake each other from the nightmare I had plunged them into.

"Or"—I jerked my head toward them—"I could simply haunt the two of you!" I widened my eyes. I gave them a crazed smile. "We could have the most delightful time together!"

"The attic!" The words sounded torn from one man's throat.

I tilted my head slowly, my smile squeezing fake blood from the corners of my mouth.

"The west attic!" the other one said as though confessing a sin.

I glanced toward where my brother was hiding. I gave him the smallest nod, telling him to go.

I was going to have a little more fun with these two. I was going to send them screaming and stumbling into the night.

LISANDRO

"EMBRY?" I BANGED on the door to the west attic.

It was locked, and the hinges wouldn't give, but I kept saying his name. He either couldn't hear me or couldn't answer.

I heard a thread of noise, rough and distant. It sounded like the way Embry coughed when leaves came from his throat.

Those myths reared up in me again. I wanted to be Eurybarus taking the garlands that marked Alcyoneus for death. I wanted to be Menestratus saving Cleostratus from an insatiable monster.

Then I remembered Menestratus's breastplate made of fishhooks. The curve of those hooks gave me an idea.

When I came back to the attic, it was with the crowbar Lola and I had used to pry holes in the plaster. This time, I didn't bother with locked doors. I went behind the walls. I crowbarred open my own doors. I climbed the scaffolding my father had helped build.

First light streamed in through the edges of the attic. Dust motes swam as thickly as plankton underwater. Wooden crates were packed in so tightly that they looked like part of the structure.

"Embry?" I dodged between them, following that coughing sound.

The light spilled in around him, so brightly that until my eyes adjusted, I could make out only the curve of his back. His body shuddered and heaved like he was crying, but he wasn't. I could hear his gasping like he was trying to stay above water.

He coughed leaves into his hands, and I waited for his breath to settle, for his body to go still. But he kept coughing. It racked through him, and more strands of leaves spilled into his palms.

That was when I saw the tangled garlands scattered around him. They looked like a ring of debris from a shipwreck, like he'd been thrown onto shore with seaweed trailing off his limbs.

Those ropes of leaves possessed him, and they weren't letting him go.

The texture of his shirt, damp from his sweat, lit a match at the back of my brain. That shirt reminded me of something. It looked as pale and worn as the flyleaves in my parents' old copy of *Metamorphoses*, the one Lola slept holding as though it were a doll. The lettering had worn off the spine, the cloth binding frayed.

And a page had nearly been torn in half because of how eagerly Lola turned through the book. It was from the story of Pygmalion and Galatea. Pygmalion was a sculptor who fell in love with his own sculpture so deeply that she became a living woman. When Pygmalion kissed Galatea's alabaster lips, he found them warm. He had wanted her to be living flesh so badly that she had come to life. And maybe something like that really could happen if you wanted something badly enough.

I wanted this boy to be able to do what he wanted with his own mouth.

I knelt in front of Embry. I kissed him, the edges of the leaves as sharp as paper on my tongue. I kissed him, and I could feel the hitch of jagged edges in my own throat. I kissed him, and it was like closing a circuit.

His body relaxed. His breath settled.

He looked at me, eyes wet and reddened.

"I told you to get out of here." His voice came rough and thin, and he said it with a sad, resigned smile.

He gently pried my fingers away from my palms, out of the fists they were clenched in.

When he opened my hands, they were full of leaves.

"I told you this place takes people," he said.

My fingers trembled, the leaves shivering in my palms.

"What happened?" I asked.

"I try to stand up to him." Embry shook his head at the seams of light coming into the attic. "And every time, I let him make me afraid. I let him turn me into a coward. Everything I want to say turns to this."

He traced his hand along the garlands. "Every time I try to fight back, this is what happens. Every time I try to tell the truth."

"What truth?" I asked.

"They were gone," he said. "They were just gone."

"Who?" I asked.

"My sisters," he said. "That's why I can't leave. This is the last place I saw them. They were here, and then they were just gone."

The way he sounded, the way he kept shaking his head, it didn't make sense. He wasn't talking like a brother who'd watched his sisters cut scandalous paths through society, denouncing their own family. He was talking like something far worse had happened and it was somehow his fault.

"Come on," I said. "Let's get you out of here."

His eyes landed on the crowbar.

He grabbed it so suddenly I thought he might swing it at me.

"He accuses me of sending them money." Embry got up off the floor. "But it's his excuse. It's his cover story to make me look crazy. Where would I even send it? It's bullshit and he knows it."

I got to my feet. I tried to figure out something to say that had a better chance of success than *Embry, put down the crowbar.*

"You ever notice that there are paintings and photos of almost everything around here?" He shoved a crate out of the way. "My father. His mother. Blythe." He shoved past another one, and another, checking the markings on the sides. "The cars. The grounds. The gardens. The flying buttresses have an oil portrait around here somewhere." He took the crowbar and pried the lid off a crate. "But ever notice something's missing?"

He stared into the crate, and his body settled. His next breath was slow and quiet. The light turned the back of his shirt translucent, and the starch on the collar made it look like a leaf of stationery.

He brushed the sawdust off the engraved metal of a picture frame. Behind the glass was an age-softened photo, the gray tone yellowing to shades of brown. It showed a broad-canopied tree, an oak maybe. The bristle of brush in the background placed it as one of the trees out in the hills. Whispers of clouds lightened what must have been a brilliant blue sky.

The tree cast shade so thick that it took me a minute to notice the figures on the boughs. Girls in patterned dresses adorned the trees like streamers. A few looked a little older than Lola and me, a couple younger. They draped themselves across the branches. Their palms rested on the wood. They propped their chins on the backs of their hands as they stared dreamily into the daylight.

"He's shoved them all up here," Embry said. "Just like he tries to do with me when I say things he doesn't like."

He pulled out another, then another. The girls' ages varied only slightly from one photo to the next, lining up with how recently The Coterie had been finished. The dresses were the latest a few seasons ago; I recognized them from Lola's magazines.

The Fairfax daughters were older girls, and they were young women, the kind Lola would have admired in advertisements. They wore dark dresses with pale polka dots, the flounces of the skirts trailing off the branches. They wore pressed shirts with neat collars, the hems tucked into heavy wool skirts. Some had their hair long and tumbling onto their shoulders. Others wore short curls as carefully set as their dark lipstick. Some were barefoot, or just in their stockings, their ankles resting against the knots in the wood. Their T-strap and two-tone dancing shoes had been flung into the wild grass below. Others still wore theirs, their French heels and center buckles hanging off the boughs.

Not one of them looked at the camera. They each stared out beyond the reach of the frames, smiling as though they all shared the same secret.

"They were here." Embry moved away from the crate. "They were here, and then they weren't."

This was why he'd stayed. This was the place where the thread of his sisters' lives had dropped. This place was what he had left of them. It was where all his questions lived.

If I were Embry, and his sisters had been Lola, I would have become part of the ground here before I left.

Embry stood in the thickening beams of light. The illuminated dust was a fine veil between him and me. His head dipped low like he was looking down at something. The sun piercing the attic turned the back of his shirt collar to a gilded ribbon.

I went to where he was standing.

"Embry," I said. "What happened to them?"

At the edge of the attic, the beams were transforming into branches, as though the wood of the house were becoming something alive again.

"He turned them into trees," Embry said. "I don't know how he did it, but he did. He turned them into things he could keep quiet and keep exactly where he wanted."

I FOUND LOLA on the roof outside the Magnificent Karina's rooms. She was still wearing her white dress, her hands and face streaked with fake blood.

When I climbed out the window, she looked up. "How's he doing?"

"Pretty wrung out." I sat down next to her, settling my weight onto the tiles. "He's asleep in there now. I didn't think he should go back to his room."

Lola wasn't looking so great herself. Whatever thrill she'd gotten scaring the daylights out of those men had already burned out. She'd pulled her knees into her chest, arms hugged around them.

"You okay?" I asked, the stupidest of questions.

The sun was low, still behind the trees, and Lola stared into the morning blue.

"I wasn't there," she said.

"What do you mean?" I asked.

She studied the edge of the roofline like she was counting tiles.

"When they were sick," she said. "I didn't help you. I didn't help them."

"You couldn't," I said. "I didn't want you to. You'd had whooping cough, what, a month before? I could still hear it in your lungs. They didn't want you near them, either. They didn't know what they had. They didn't know if you could get it."

"I know, I know." She angled slightly away from me. "But that's why I wanted to do all this. Because I didn't do anything then. I wanted to make it a little bit right even though it can never be right. I wanted to win after everything we lost."

My heart hadn't buckled in half this hard, this fast, since that day at the carnival.

Lola's voice had the tinge of both laughing and crying as she said, "You must hate me."

"I do not hate you," I said. "I love you. And even if I didn't love you, I'd pretend I did because you are maybe the last person on earth whose bad side I'd ever want to be on."

In profile, I could see Lola almost smiling. Just for a second. Then it was gone again.

"But I did this," she said. "We're here because of me. I did all of this."

"Right," I said. "You did all of this. You set all of this up for us. Do you know how impressive that is?"

She angled her head back toward me, just a little.

"I know you wanted revenge, but I also know that's not all this was about," I said. "You wanted something that even remotely resembled justice. You wanted life to look different for us."

"Yeah, and it's going really well, isn't it?" Lola pulled something out of her pocket. "Here." She set a folded photograph in my hand. "Maybe you can give this back to him for me."

I unfolded it, revealing a small version of the kind of photograph Embry had just shown me. It captured his sisters looking like they were growing out of tree boughs. In this one, they all wore the liquid fabric and heavy embellishment of evening gowns.

"Where did you get this?" I asked.

"Trust me," Lola said. "Even if I told you, it wouldn't help."

She was quiet for a minute.

"Embry's right, you know," Lola said. "About what Fairfax did to his sisters."

"How do you know?" I said.

"Trust me," she said. "I know."

The dangerous thing at The Coterie had never been Embry. He'd been declared dangerous for trying to name what he saw.

"He's going to win," Lola said. "Again. Fairfax is going to win, and nothing will change."

"It doesn't have to be that way," I said, because I wanted it to be true. I was talking ahead of my own problem-solving, because right now all I was seeing were problems.

"How do we help Embry?" Lola shrugged toward the open window. "How do we help ourselves?"

A streak of fake blood on her neck caught the light. The start of an idea made a sound in my brain, like the friction of a match strike.

"Maybe we can't do anything to Fairfax on our own," I said. "But maybe we can if we're not the only ones who know what he's done."

Lola looked at me.

"It's a lot easier to defeat a monster if everyone else sees him for what he is," I said.

"How do we make sure they do?" she asked.

I smiled. "We scare Fairfax into admitting it."

"You have my attention." Lola sat up straighter. "But how exactly do we do that?"

"We enact your plan." I smiled at her. "I'm the menacing brown boy ghost. And I'm coming for his soul."

LOLA

THIS EARLY IN the morning, The Coterie was quiet. Except for the kitchens. The bakers were preparing dough. The chefs were planning out the day's menus and verifying the seating charts. And in the small auxiliary kitchen, Hayden was water-spotting glasses from last night.

"Want a hand?" I asked.

Hayden looked over his shoulder, jumped, and almost dropped a highball.

"What are you doing?" He was breathing hard. "What are you wearing?"

"Sorry." I'd gone to find him so quickly that I'd forgotten about the greenish-white pancake makeup and the fake blood. "I just needed to talk to you."

"Well, then why didn't you pop out of a dark corner? Or jump out of a closet?" He finished drying the glass. "Is there an upcoming horror theme party I need to know about?"

I shut the door behind me. "Do you remember how I told

you that if you knew everything about me you wouldn't want to be anywhere near me, and you said 'Try me'?"

"If you literally scare me to death, I might change my mind," he said. "But yes, I remember. I meant it."

"Well"—I fidgeted my fingers together—"let's test that theory, shall we?"

I told him everything, talking while I polished glass after glass as though this would be insurance against him hating me. I told him what I had said that was true—the no-grieving-families rule, my name, washing glasses at hotels, my wonder at finding the second Iphis in the pages of Papá's book. I told him what I had said that was a lie—where my brother was, that the Magnificent Karina was my invention to begin with, the entirety of the hauntings.

I told him what had happened to our family, how I had come to The Coterie to collect some fraction of what Lisandro and I were owed.

"So do you hate me yet?" I asked once I'd gotten it all out.

Hayden's smile was half reassurance, half challenge. "Not yet."

When I introduced Hayden and my brother, he offered Hayden an apologetic hand. "I'm Lisandro."

"Ah, yes," Hayden said. "The priest."

"Only during select Wednesday matinees," Lisandro said.

This was how Hayden, Embry, my brother, and I ended up in the attic together, staring at the branches braiding themselves into the house.

"It wasn't like this until last night," Embry said.

"How often are you up here?" I asked.

"This is where my father has them put me when I start saying things he doesn't like," Embry said.

"If he doesn't like what you're saying, why hasn't he sent you away?" Hayden asked.

"Because he doesn't want me saying those things to other people." Embry stared at the interlacing pattern reaching across the attic floor. "If I'm here, he can at least keep an eye on me."

In some places, the strands were as knotted and dense as roots. In others, they grew as delicately as vines. They crossed over one another as intricately as drawings of veins in an anatomy book.

Their pattern mirrored the vines crossing my skin.

Hayden crouched, studying the thinnest strands. They looked fastened together with fibers that resembled fraying rope. They were dark, but the angles of the sun turned some reddish or gold.

Hair. It was hair growing in with the vines and roots and branches. Some curled around the wood. Some wound into a coil like the twist of a bun. Some braided together like a plait trailing down a girl's back.

All those stories my brother and I had heard growing up, and yet it had never occurred to me. No one knew where exactly the Fairfax sisters were because they were still here. They were dryads, transformed into oak trees. They were nymphs turned into willows, elms, apple trees. They were the Heliades, mourning something so deeply that their bodies became poplars and their tears became amber. They were Clytie or Leucothoe, blossoms or frankincense trees finding the light after their father tried to bury them alive.

"If he did this to them," Lisandro asked Embry, "why didn't he do the same to you?"

"I don't know." Embry gave Lisandro a smile that was sad but came with the edge of something sharp. I recognized that look. I'd seen it in Lisandro, the embers of a defiance that he'd tried to destroy in himself but that hadn't completely gone out. "Maybe there's only so much scandal one family name can withstand. My father decided he could weather a mistress but not a divorce. Maybe he thought rebellious daughters were something he could write off, but a vanished son would make things look a lot worse. Me being here makes things almost look normal."

To anyone else, the way my brother set a hand on Embry's shoulder might have just seemed like a comforting gesture. But my brother didn't casually touch people like that, especially other boys. I should have hated this, the way Lisandro's fingers brushed the edge of Embry's collarbone. I should have hated my brother breathing the same air as a Fairfax.

But it all looked different now. I'd seen Embry cowering away from his father. I'd seen him coughing cords of leaves into his hands.

Maybe Fairfax hadn't turned him into a tree like his sisters, but he'd left him this awful fate. Embry had to live among what was left of his sisters. He had to live with the truth turning to leaves on his tongue.

The wood creaked and groaned. The beams were splitting along their grains. The vines and branches were squeezing and warping the rafters, growing deeper into the house, trying to take it apart.

The wood of my spine felt as electrically charged as my heart. The vines on my skin were the start of a hundred trees.

My muscles were weaving themselves into branches. I had a forest inside me.

"My brother said you wanted to do something about what your father did to our family," I told Embry. "What he did to a lot of families. Did you mean it?"

"Yes," Embry said. He looked at me more unflinchingly than he had since meeting me.

"My brother and I have a plan," I said. "But we'd need your help." I looked between Hayden and Embry. "Both of you. Do you think you can get us some dry ice?"

"Is that a serious question?" Hayden said. "Of course I can."

"Good." I looked back at Embry. "By the time we're done, everyone's going to know what kind of man your father really is."

The resolve on Embry's face wavered. "I can't. I want to say it, but I never can. I've never been able to."

"You're not going to say it." I tilted my head toward my brother. "He's going to get them to say it."

My brother's smile back at me lit a thousand yellow flares. We could do this. We were the Bernal siblings. We knew how to turn solid ground into trapdoors.

LOLA

"I'VE BEEN THINKING over what you said." All it took was slipping it into conversation over midmorning tea. "About the awful feeling you had coming here. About how Mr. Fairfax disregarded it."

The black enamel cup in Blythe's hand went still.

"The ghost and I have been building a strong rapport." I laced a ribbon of honey into my tea. "We've made a great deal of progress. He's a very closed, very guarded young man. But he's opened up to me in ways that would have seemed almost impossible when I first arrived. And I think he's trying to warn you."

Blythe set down her cup. "Warn me?" The gold trim gleamed as the cup clattered against the saucer. "About what?"

"It's difficult to tell." I stirred my tea casually, as though I was recounting a scandal in a distant town. "But from what he's said and what I've sensed, there's an otherworldly conflict ensuing. Invisible to us, of course. But I believe the young man is on your side and that he wishes to warn you of malevolent forces"—I circled my hands on either side of Blythe's head—"whirling around you."

Blythe knotted her gloved fingers together. "What sort of forces?"

"I'm not entirely sure." I made my face dreamy and regretful. "But I think it has something to do with the girl who's been frightening a few of the guests."

"So it's true?" Blythe asked. "She's real."

"I was skeptical myself," I said. "The power of suggestion and all. But now that I've investigated more closely, I have a stronger sense of her and her dark feminine energy."

The word *dark* was honey in my mouth. Sweet to my tongue, but frightening to Blythe and her guests. To them, *dark* meant evil and vicious. To my brother and me, *dark* meant the life we carried in our blood and in the colors of our bodies. To us, *dark* was the cupped palms of the night sky, holding all the stars.

"The frightening occurrences around here," I said. "I believe we might find their cause in that conflict between the spirits."

"Really?" The ruffled coral of Blythe's sleeves betrayed the shiver going through her.

"Oh, yes," I said. "That dark feminine energy seeks to incite chaos, and the young man does all he can in order to fight that chaos. He wishes to protect you. And between you and me"—I leaned close enough to smell the powdery scent of Blythe's perfume—"I've been getting the strong sense that he's ready to communicate with you. All of you."

Those last words infused a thrill into Blythe's worry. Her eyes opened a little wider.

"In fact"—I closed my eyes—"I believe he wants to address

you all tonight. I believe he wishes to speak to you regarding how you all might help him in stemming the tide of that dark chaos. Do you think you could assemble everyone tonight?"

"Yes, of course," Blythe said.

"Outside, I think," I said, "in the gardens, in the very realm that the dark feminine energy believes she rules." I opened my eyes and set a palm over Blythe's hands. "Might I make a truly unfair request?"

"Anything," Blythe said.

I leaned in even closer. "Please don't tell Mr. Fairfax why you're gathering the guests. Not just yet."

"But why?" Blythe asked.

"I fear he's amused by all this," I said. "I fear he does not truly want the spiritual presences to move on. It's almost as though"—I hesitated, and Blythe leaned forward, waiting—"all this is entertainment to him."

There was an edge to Blythe's expression now, a simmering rage. I had spoken aloud the very thing she feared.

If I could turn Blythe against Fairfax, we'd be halfway there.

Blythe didn't even need to lie to Fairfax. The Coterie was always ready for a party. When she asked everyone to dress their best for a moonlight soiree, no one questioned it.

While Blythe directed the placement of floral arrangements and candelabras, the four of us passed in and out of the shadows. Lisandro and Embry set up the lamps. Hayden and I hid banks of dry ice like little snowdrifts.

"You're sure you want to do this?" I asked Hayden. "If this works, you won't have a job anymore."

"None of us will," Hayden said. "But if we do this right, we'll squeeze some impressive severance payments out of old

Fairfax. He won't be able to afford a single word more of bad publicity, including from his former staff."

"I look forward to it." The right strap of my dress fell down my arm. This gown was another from the Magnificent Karina's collection. I'd chosen it for the way the color shifted as I moved, how the skirt looked almost liquid. But it was turning out to be more trouble than it was worth. The fabric was slick enough that the straps kept sliding around. I could imagine Margaret Drummond's smirk, her satisfaction at how I couldn't wear her clothes as well as she could.

"You know, you never told me." I moved the strap back into place. "How did you learn to bartend? Are you even old enough to drink?"

"According to my paperwork, absolutely." Hayden turned through the tablecloths I'd pilfered, looking for one the right size. "According to God and the truth, absolutely not. But I knew what I was doing from day one, so that helped."

"How?" I asked.

He unfurled one of the tablecloths. "A lot of drinkers in my family. Happy drunks, mostly. Not so happy the rest of the time. But positively jovial when they have a full glass in their hands. So I learned early."

He said it without flinching; the memory was something he kept close enough to look at but far enough that it wouldn't touch him. He'd done what we all did when we were small. He'd figured out how to make his world safer. He'd worked out what spells held the right kind of magic to make everything warmer and calmer. He'd been a little sorcerer, stirring potions into highball glasses.

As we draped the tablecloth over the dry ice, the strap of

my dress slipped again. The evening air skimmed my shoulder blades.

Hayden paused.

He was at the perfect angle to see the knobs of my spine and close enough to see the texture, how the wood had broken through to the surface.

"Lola," he said slowly. He sounded as though I had a tarantula on my back and he was about to tell me not to make sudden movements.

I could have conned him. I could have said, *What? What is it?* I could have pretended that what he was seeing was news to me.

But I couldn't lie to this boy anymore.

I met his eyes. It was as good as admitting everything.

"Lola," Hayden said, his voice thinned out. "Does your brother know?"

I stood back up. "Do you think he'd be doing this if he did?"

"And why do you think that is?" Hayden asked. "What happened to Embry's sisters, what if the same thing happens to you?"

"I can't back down now," I said. "Not after all this."

"Yes, you can." Hayden slid his fingers onto my cheek. His hand was cool from being near the dry ice. "You don't have to do this. You don't have to risk that happening to you."

"That's exactly it," I said. "If I back down, this is what happens to me. Look at the stories in your book. Someone's always trying to turn girls into something that will put them in their place. Sisters who get in the way of the gods' plans. Daughters who don't do what their fathers want. Girls who fall in love when they're not supposed to and who don't fall in love when someone wants them to. They get turned into trees, or flowers, or birds, and that's supposed to be the end of the story, but I'm not letting it be the end of mine."

Hayden's jaw tensed as he checked the edges of the cloth, making sure no vapor was escaping.

"Her name means violet flower," he said.

"Whose name?" I asked.

"Ianthe," Hayden said. "That name means violet flower. But she doesn't turn into one. It's just her name. Not everyone who falls in love in a way they're not supposed to ends up turned into something they're not. Not everyone who does something a way they're not supposed to ends up as something other than themselves."

I kissed his jawline. He almost relaxed how he was holding it.

"I'll take that as a vote of confidence," I said.

By the time the stars were out, music was playing from silver Victor Vs. The staff had draped shimmering fabric from what was left of the pillars. At Blythe's direction, Hayden mixed cocktails flecked with gold leaf.

Men donned formal jackets in satin and velvet. Women strolled the terraces in new gowns, blush in the latest shade of lavender draping their cheeks. Guests milled around the pool in their finery, marveling at the forest growing out of the water.

Embry was making his well-behaved appearance, his shirt and suit pressed. Everyone had heard about what they called his latest *outburst.* Every wife of every industry baron was touching his arm, asking, "Are you feeling better?" The lightning of my anger flashed through my blood every time he had to smile politely and say, "Much, thank you."

When the party was well underway, Blythe made her entrance, wearing a gown she'd been saving the whole season.

The underskirt was sapphire velvet, and the color showed through the delicate frost of the skirt's overlay. The sleeves were stiff with silver embellishments; she'd told me the threads were wrapped in real silver. She'd had her money sewn into her gown, and it gleamed across her shoulders as she, too, touched Embry's arm and asked, "Are you feeling any better?"

"I am." The smile he produced for her landed between tired and docile. "Thank you for asking."

I nodded to Hayden at the bar. He signaled my brother, who then, out of sight, would pull the cloths off the first banks of dry ice.

A minute later, Lisandro appeared at the edge of the landscaped gardens.

His posture and the makeup I'd put on him gave him a tired and tormented look, as though he'd been wrestling with malevolent forces. Hidden lamps surrounded him with an aura of moon-green. A thick, cold mist rose not just at his back but around him. Hayden had lined Lisandro's coat pockets, insulating them so the dry ice could release its vapor without burning or freezing him.

The first gasps rose up from the crowd.

As slowly as a sleepwalker, I approached him. I moved through the bordering gardens and into the rough grass of the hillsides.

Behind me came the footsteps of curious guests. But they paused at the edge of the landscaped grounds. They seemed as apprehensive as if they were about to step into a dark river.

My brother waited, the illuminated boy, haunted and haunting. The iridescent green light gave the usual warm brown of his skin a cold and unearthly cast.

"Will you speak to us?" I asked him.

He nodded once, silently.

"What is it you've come to say?" I asked.

Lisandro looked past me, straight at Bixby Fairfax.

"The sickness," he said. "It was here, and you knew it. Yet you ordered everyone to keep building."

I couldn't tell exactly what flashed across Fairfax's expression. Calculation, maybe. Strategy. Offense that anyone, living or dead, would speak to him this way.

"What does he mean?" Blythe drew close to Fairfax. Her confusion almost seemed genuine. It lined her face. It dampened her beauty. It wasn't an expression she would have done on purpose.

"The influenza," my brother said. "It was sweeping through, and yet you insisted everyone stay."

"Is that true?" Blythe asked Fairfax.

The dry ice vapor spun a luminous cloud around my brother.

"Unburden your soul," he said.

Murmurs came up from the crowd.

"What is it he means?" I turned to Fairfax. "Have you anything to confess?"

"No," Fairfax said. "Nothing."

How believably he said it was a chilled knife through the air. His confusion was so calm.

"Lies only fuel the malevolent spirits," Lisandro said, the cold fog of death at his back.

"I assure you, I've never done anything to endanger anyone." Fairfax didn't hide from my brother. He was even drawing toward the front of the crowd, addressing them all like a politician. "But if any underhanded deed has been carried out on my watch, I give you my word, we will find the culprit."

Bixby Fairfax said his lines as cleanly as if he was in a play.

A cloud bank of vapor filled the space between the trees.

Risk is a flower that blooms, Mamá said, *and its season, mija, is whenever you're sure you've thought of everything.*

And we should have thought of this: Guilt didn't work on those who truly thought they'd done nothing wrong. Appeals to the immortal soul had no effect on men who could commit a thousand sins and insist it was for the greater good. There was no speaking to the conscience of someone who thought they'd only taken what was their due.

Bixby Fairfax could lie perfectly, and everyone would believe it because he believed it. Of course it wasn't his fault that the building was falling apart; shouldn't skilled craftsmen have been able to build his resort as fast as he wanted? Of course he hadn't led workers to their deaths; how could it be his fault if they'd died months after returning home? Of course spirits and their tales of the afterlife held no fear for men like Fairfax; to them, the only gods were themselves. To them, the only afterlife was the fine figures they would cut in the history books.

Guilt or doubt didn't show on Blythe's face, either. She might have faulted him for not listening to her, but that, it seemed, was as far as her doubt would go. She could not entertain the idea that Fairfax had wronged people whose names she didn't even know. She couldn't reconcile such harm with the man who'd given her a closet full of silk and a dressing table stuffed with jewels.

"What about my sisters?" Embry asked.

The crowd seemed to inhale together.

Embry was looking more at Blythe than his father as he said, "You know what happened. You were there."

We all stared at Fairfax and Blythe. Lisandro. Embry. Hayden. Me. The rest of the crowd.

"Those girls showed no gratitude for anything," Fairfax said. He managed to sound regretful, pitying, rather than angry.

"They had to watch you make our mother accept your affair," Embry said.

"We were in love," Blythe said.

"Wonderful." Sarcasm frosted Embry's words. "Then be in love. Get married. But he wouldn't give our mother a divorce."

"You know that was as much for your mother as anyone," Fairfax said. "A divorce would have looked even worse for her than for me."

"You didn't want to let her have her own life," Embry said. "You wouldn't let her pursue her own happiness in peace. You wouldn't even let us live with her. You wanted us here so you could show us off as a matched set. You wanted it to look like we were all on your side."

The photographs Embry had shown us ticked through my brain like images from a projector. I could imagine his sisters lined up at their father's command. Fairfax would have been delighted to dazzle his friends and business acquaintances with their beauty, their wit, the colors of their hair and eyes as varied as the seasons. Fairfax would have wanted them here at The Coterie, this extravagant resort he'd built as a monument to himself.

He would have wanted to show them off as collected objects.

"And they complied," Embry said. "That was the worst part. I had to watch them. And I hated them for it. I hated them until I found out"—Embry's throat tightened, cutting off the end of his sentence.

"How could you hate them?" Fairfax gave Embry the same calm smile he'd given me in his study. "You've always been just like them."

"Now, that's not fair." Blythe was getting more worked up than Fairfax. "He isn't." She put a hand on the sleeve of Fairfax's dinner jacket. "I've told you he isn't."

Fairfax barely seemed to notice Blythe.

"You're just like them." Fairfax moved closer to Embry. The guests drew back to clear his path. "Every day you're becoming more like them."

Under his father's stare, Embry's shoulders rounded. His back shuddered, and his breathing sounded so choked and damp I could almost feel the leaves in my own throat.

LISANDRO

EMBRY WAS CRUMBLING under his father's words. And his own words were turning to leaves and vines in his throat.

The guests had been staring at Fairfax, but now they were watching Embry.

According to rumor, Embry was a troubled boy. A dangerous boy. And if everyone saw what was about to happen, he'd be worse off than before. They'd consider him possessed by the same malevolent spirits ripping The Coterie apart.

Everyone would see it, that rope of leaves like a garland. I wanted to take it from him as badly as I wanted to help Lola tear this place to pieces. I wanted to take it from him because it didn't matter if I looked possessed to everyone. To everyone, I was already dead. To everyone, I was already the spirit of a brown boy. To everyone, I was already dangerous twice over.

At the back of my brain, those leaves twisted into a wreath. They became the garland Eurybarus lifted from Alcyoneus's head.

Maybe I could take the thing that was stopping Embry from speaking.

As I came toward Embry, everyone else drew back, even Fairfax.

Embry's surprise at my approach must have looked like fear to everyone else. I was shrouded in cold mist. I carried the chill of death.

As I reached out to touch him, gasps lifted off the crowd like the vapor from my pockets.

I set my hands on either side of Embry's face.

When Pygmalion kissed the alabaster lips of his sculpture, he found them warm. Pygmalion had wanted Galatea to be living flesh so badly that she had come to life.

But no one had asked Galatea if she wanted it.

I brushed my thumbs over Embry's lips, asking the question with my fingers. If I did this, it would make him a boy everyone considered touched by death.

He held his throat tight. But his slight nod was enough, so I put my lips against his.

The dark star in the center of me carried everything I knew. Boys like me did not live, and if we lived, it did not end well for us. The rustling of river reeds reminded me that Calamus and Carpus had drowned during their swimming contest. The wild bouquets Lola gathered in spring reminded me of Apollo and Hyacinthus and the blood that turned to purple-blue flowers. Even if Achilles and Patroclus had not lived in the midst of war, they would have been doomed by the cant of their own hearts.

I could not love without carrying death with me.

As I kissed Embry, I felt the sharp edges under his tongue.

I felt them growing into my body instead of his so that he could speak.

Then that feeling vanished from under my tongue, and the sensation of leaves filled my hands.

Embry and I drew back from each other. The air between us felt as alive as the motion blur in a photograph.

We looked down at our hands. A rope of laurel leaves was gathered in his palms and coiled around the backs of my knuckles. We were holding the same tangled garland.

Embry looked at me like I'd torn him open and found a galaxy inside him.

I had marked him, and he had marked me, and these leaves marked us both. We were both Alcyoneus. We were both Eurybarus. Our shared fate was to face the waiting monsters.

LOLA

EMBRY HELD THE rope of leaves as surely as a weapon. He didn't flinch from his father. He faced him straight on, eyes up.

"I am like them." He looked at Fairfax. "I'm exactly like them."

There was a shift in Fairfax's expression. It was as fast and small as a mosquito crossing in front of a lamp, but I caught it, something throwing him off. Then it was gone. He recovered, and a smile broke over his face.

"You." Fairfax shook a finger at Embry. But it wasn't a gesture of accusation or anger. He was still smiling. "All of you. You've set this all up, haven't you?" He turned the shaking of his finger toward me. "You found this marvelous girl all so you could pull this stupendous prank on me, didn't you?"

The words sounded so genuine I couldn't tell if he believed them. When it came to lies, he was a better showman than my brother and me combined.

"They fooled us!" He put an arm around Blythe. "Didn't

they fool us?" He looked back at Embry. "I must say, I'm proud." He clapped once, the ultimate good sport. "I didn't know you had it in you. Or did your sisters help you with the whole thing?" With gleeful expectation, he looked over each shoulder. "Are they around here somewhere?"

His performance was convincing enough to put the guests at ease. Their laughter was small and hesitant but relieved.

Lisandro's, Hayden's, and Embry's faces reflected the shock I felt. Fairfax was going to play all of this off as a joke. With a good-natured laugh, he was stripping away the weight of everything we had.

"And you." Fairfax turned back to me. "Who here will ever be amused by a sleight-of-hand trick after witnessing your brilliant show?" He gestured toward me like I was a circus act. "Shall we show the young lady our gratitude?"

The guests applauded, sighing with amusement and the relief of now being in on the joke.

Hayden had the most exhausted *Are you kidding me?* look I'd ever seen. Embry looked as though the gravity holding his heart together was giving out.

My brother stared at Fairfax with more rage than I thought he had in him. Lisandro had unlocked Embry's mouth, and still Fairfax had managed to speak over him fast enough to write the story the way he wanted it to go.

"Young lady"—Fairfax strolled up to me, Blythe at his side—"you have my respect. And believe me"—he held out his hand to me—"I don't give it easily."

He didn't just want to cover this over. He wanted me to take his hand in front of everyone and help him do it. I wished I were strong enough to crush every bone in that hand. I wished I could melt the rings off his fingers. I wished

I were smart enough or big enough to do something other than let everything crumble. But all I had was my rage, and it was worthless for anything except transforming my bones into branches.

Fairfax's words rang in my head.

You're just like them.

But then the echo of Embry's words followed.

I am like them.

I'm exactly like them.

A current went through me like a shimmer of warm air on a cold night. But it wasn't from the air. It was the ground under me. It came up through my body and streamed out of my back, like the drawings I'd seen of solar winds. I could feel the Fairfax sisters' defiance in my own heart. It was blazing light. It was a magnetic field coming up from the ground, and their story came up from the ground with it.

For a minute, it was mine, too. For a minute, I was all of them at once, and I saw everything.

I saw Embry watching his sisters, a few of us older than he was, a couple younger, but all of us glittering with secrets that made us seem beyond his reach. I saw him staring up at us as we draped ourselves on tree boughs. I saw him watching us from windows as we stayed in the trees past midnight, the moon silvering our hair.

When he asked us why we didn't come in to sleep, we showed him our secrets, like slipping pressed flowers from between the pages of a book. We showed him the flowering buds on the ends of our eyelashes, like caught snowflakes. We showed him the rings around our belly buttons like tree knots. We showed him our fingernails patterned like the veins of leaves.

How? he asked us, breathless with wonder. *How do you do that?*

We smiled and whispered, *Anyone can be anything.*

We did not look like girls who could blur our bodies together with trees. We weren't barefoot nymphs in Pre-Raphaelite gowns, flaxen hair rippling to our waists. We were girls with dark lipstick, polished T-strap shoes, and vicious smiles. We were girls with our hair carefully set, blush on our cheeks, nail lacquer giving our claws a dark shine. We were as chic as hotel lobbies, yet we were inseparable from the rugged, drought-hardened trees in the hills.

As a little boy, Embry had adored us.

Until, in one shared motion, we turned our backs on our mother.

Or so he thought.

Embry loathed our compliance with Fairfax and Blythe. He detested the way we lined ourselves up like antique figurines every time our father wanted to impress someone. Worst of all, we complimented The Coterie, this monument to Fairfax's new life even though on paper he hadn't even let go of his old one. We praised the shoddy and rushed construction. We praised the crumbling walls and uneven joists.

Embry's disdain for us, his deepening sense of betrayal, would not leave him alone. It kept him from sleeping.

So when he heard us sneaking out of our rooms at night, he followed us.

He found us in corners of the under-construction building. Our lacquered fingernails grabbed at the edges of the wallpaper. Our wicked hands pried up just-installed floorboards. We ripped away carved paneling and antique corbels.

We could not tear apart the walls themselves, but any pretty detailing we could dismantle, we did.

We were getting vengeance for our mother and for ourselves. We smiled to our father's face by day and took his palace apart by night. We left him flummoxed as to why things were wearing so badly, falling apart so quickly.

We knew Embry was there, watching us. But for almost a week, he was too timid to approach us. When he did, he found us in the indoor swimming pool, all of us prying tiny blue and gold tiles off the walls. We gathered them into our hands and threw them into the water like tinkling glass confetti.

Embry joined us, filling his own hands with broken color. He pried away carved decorative borders, throwing the pieces out into the hills like he could give the wood back. He sabotaged the pool pumps; within weeks the steel heat exchanger and cast-iron pump corroded so much they were as soft as cheese.

We had never been prouder.

One night, we asked him, *Do you really want to help us?*

And even though he was fifteen, he'd nodded up at us with the wide eyes of the little boy we'd once known him as. He'd looked as young as when he'd first watched us in the trees, our shadows crossing the ground.

We relished the nocturnal thrill of taking The Coterie apart with our brother. But it hadn't gotten us what we wanted. That was where Embry would come in.

He would place himself outside Blythe's suite. He would make sure he was noisy enough to wake Blythe, a light sleeper who kept her own private rooms to escape Fairfax's snoring.

Embry would lead her right to us, so she could catch us all in the act.

We thought Blythe would crumble like the tiles off the walls. We thought she would wake our father. She would cry to him that these horrible, deceitful girls and their traitor of a brother were ruining their beautiful resort, that we weren't worth the trouble, that it was really time to send us all off to our mother, wasn't it?

The scene didn't play as we meant it to.

Embry didn't reach us in time. He must have gone down a wrong hallway, taken a wrong staircase. He didn't join us in the destruction quickly enough. By the time Blythe caught up with him, she thought he'd been trying to lead her to what we'd been doing. She thought he'd been trying to show her why construction was going so badly.

You're a good one, Embry, Blythe had said. Her hands on his shoulders had held him in place. She stopped him from going into the indoor pool where we were scraping away handfuls of tiles.

You're the only one your father and I can trust, Blythe whispered.

But I didn't—

Blythe shushed him. *I know you don't want to get them in trouble.*

But I've been—

This must have been so hard for you. But you did the right thing.

But it was my fault. It's not them. It's really me. I—

Shh, you don't have to take the blame for them.

No matter what he said, Blythe cut him off. His own words

withered in his throat. He earned permanent favor with Blythe, and it was poison on the back of his tongue.

For a minute, I was one of the Fairfax daughters. I was there, in the remote, unfinished corner of the house where Fairfax and Blythe decided to lock us until morning, when they would decide what to do with us next.

We heard Fairfax and Blythe outside the locked door.

If you'd just let me talk to them, Blythe said, *I'm sure we could sort this all out.*

There's no talking to them, Fairfax said. *There never has been. They're like their mother. But they'll turn on each other in there. You watch. Without their lipsticks and their magazines, with nothing to do but point fingers, they'll turn on each other. By morning, they'll be as agreeable as spaniels.*

We could sense Embry searching for us in the dark. But he could not find us in the enormous, unknowable house.

In this minute, my heart was the same as the Fairfax sisters'. We wanted out of that attic, that house, those lives. We wanted it badly enough that our limbs stretched into roots. I felt my own fingers becoming the kind of vines that spread wild across the hillsides. I felt the raw will that could turn our bodies into the growing things we'd loved since we were small.

We broke away from The Coterie while destroying more of it on the way out. We left Fairfax and Blythe mystified about how we'd escaped the locked room, breaking the beams apart as we vanished.

I was one of them, the Fairfax daughters. I was livid and unyielding and more willing to become something else than to stay where I was.

The next morning, we were gone. But we were close enough

to hear our brother's questions. Everything he asked was met with insistence not to speak of us.

It'll only upset Blythe, Fairfax said.

It'll only upset your father, Blythe said.

Embry asked where we were.

They're with your mother, Fairfax said.

We weren't.

They're off on a wonderful trip, Blythe said. *Young ladies should have grand tours, too, shouldn't they? It's essential for becoming cultured.*

Embry could smell the bitter pith of the lie.

What do you say you and I plan one? Blythe grabbed his hands like he was a child. *We could go on a marvelous adventure next spring.*

Blythe's voice from years ago faded.

The world as it was now shifted back into place.

Fairfax was in front of me, hand still outstretched. Everything from the Fairfax daughters had rushed into me within seconds. But it was enough seconds that Fairfax's upper lip was twisting with annoyance that I was making him wait. It was almost the same look I'd seen him give Embry.

What had been happening to Embry wasn't because he was afraid.

It wasn't because he was a coward.

It was because he was exactly like his sisters.

Without knowing it, Embry had held a shard of their defiance inside him. It hadn't been fear of his father that turned Embry's words to leaves. It had been part of him that wanted to answer his father's force in the same way his sisters had. His sisters would have cheered Embry on. His sisters would have wanted him to spit the leaves into their father's face.

This was why Fairfax thought Embry was stealing to send money to his sisters, because Fairfax truly didn't know where they were. They had eluded him. They could be anywhere. As far as Fairfax knew, they had vanished into thin air.

Embry's sisters had been with him, trying to back him up. They were in his blood.

And now I could feel them lighting up mine.

My rage wasn't worthless. The Fairfax daughters had shown me how much their own had been worth.

It was only consuming me because of how desperately I'd been trying to lock it inside me.

This time, when I smiled at Bixby Fairfax, every bit of it was genuine. I shook his hand so enthusiastically that the guests cheered.

Then I held on to it.

I kept smiling.

My rage was still a living thing. It was powerful enough to transform the cells of my own body. And it was poison enough that as I gripped Bixby Fairfax's hand, I could feel it streaming into him.

Fear dampened his jovial expression. He tried to pull his hand away, but it was frozen in my grip.

The heat of my rage rushed from my hand to his. This was the gift I would leave him, courtesy of his own daughters.

I watched for the first signs of him becoming a tree. A vein sprouting leaves. A bone becoming a knot of wood. A limb transforming into a bough.

But he was turning paler. So was Blythe as she clung to him harder. They were growing impossibly pale, like the marble around us.

The fear on their faces turned to shock, and as I understood what I was seeing, my expression mirrored theirs.

Before they'd died, my parents had become living statues, all because of what Fairfax had demanded of them. But it was Fairfax himself who wanted to be as immortal as a monument, preserved in every history book.

Now the shimmering wrath of the Fairfax daughters flowed through me. Together, we were giving Bixby Fairfax exactly what he wanted.

The wave of bone white swept over not only their skin but their clothes. Fairfax's hand turned polished and impossibly smooth, like the alabaster figurines I'd stolen.

"Bixby," Blythe said, the word panicked and breathless. But she didn't let him go even as the pale wash climbed up her throat. She held to him right up to the last moments of them both turning.

They were two exquisite statues, clothed in marble garb, a startled king with a beseeching queen clinging to his arm. And the trees seemed to breathe out as though they'd never seen a more breathtaking sculpture.

I drew my hand back from those marble fingers.

I looked over my shoulder at the transfixed guests.

The sight of my face broke them out of their trance. Half of them fled right then, as though any of them might be next.

Those who stayed didn't stay for long.

In so many of the myths Mamá and Papá told us, girls became trees. Bark spread up their legs. Their necks turned to heartwood. Their arms sprouted branches. Their hair turned to leaves.

Now it was happening backward. Wispy leaves became

eyelashes. Buds of new growth transformed into the jagged white of back teeth. Fingernails patterned the bark of trunks. Acorns took on the shine of watching eyes. A quarter-moon smile flashed at the edge of a tree's hollow.

Boughs grew arms. Branches grew fingers. And they were reaching out toward all of us. Not as though they wanted our help. I knew that from the crescent-moon smiles appearing and disappearing like fireflies.

Branches wound out of my spine. Roots grew from my heels like my veins were searching for water in the ground. My anklebones turned to knots of wood. Vines twisted out of my collarbone. Each time I blinked, more of my eyelashes were the delicate stems of new blossoms.

I was meeting them halfway. We were all becoming half human, half tree, like Daphne mid-transformation. We were Bernal daughters, and we were Fairfax daughters, and we wanted everyone's fear. We wanted to taste it on our hidden tongues.

My heart became a handful of embers. It glittered so brightly that the coins in my dress were sparking. I was Circe, drawing in a breath before poisoning the sea and breaking apart the world.

I could hear Papá's voice, reading to us from those stories, and Mamá's, telling us tales her parents had told her. How all the stars were different colors and how the sun had chosen gold for itself. How daughters became islands or seabirds to escape fathers who would use them as bargaining chips. A fox that could never be caught, a dog that could catch anything it pursued, the impossibility of the two existing in the same universe, their inevitable transformation into stone the moment they met.

I imagined their voices telling our stories. A brother and a sister who'd learned to be ghosts. A boy who dreamed of Iphis and Ianthe. A boy who missed his sisters badly enough that his own heart had wandered away from his body. And a king and queen who'd become the most exquisite statues in their own collection.

LISANDRO

EMBRY HAD TOLD me about first light, the initial use of a newly built telescope. How the image seldom amounted to anything on its own. How collecting that light let astronomers calibrate the way they were seeing things.

In the days after everyone else left, we were calibrating, all of us. I wasn't an apparition. Embry wasn't the dangerous boy he'd been made into. We were recognizing each other's bodies, each adjusting the lens through which our own hands observed the other.

Every time he kissed me, we were written with light. I believed impossible things. I believed that sometimes Calamus and Carpus did not drown. Sometimes Hyacinthus did not shed his blood into flowers. Sometimes Achilles and Patroclus survived. Sometimes boys like me and Embry Fairfax became stories other than how we were lost.

Hayden was always in men's clothes now, letting my sister fine-tune the details of his hair or his tie knots with a patience she'd never gotten from me. This was where Hayden was getting used to living as the boy he was. He was learning to move through the world with the tentative hope of becoming who he'd always been.

Lola seemed as though she'd always been one of the Fairfax daughters. Sometimes she was half girl, half tree. Sometimes she joined them when they draped themselves from the wide oak boughs. Sometimes she appeared from the trees, and I wouldn't be able to tell if she'd emerged from the trunks themselves or if it had been an illusion made by shadows. She would touch my shoulder and smile, and I wouldn't know where she'd come from.

I watched her as she joined them in the work of taking the house apart. Sometimes they used their hands, sometimes their branches and roots. I watched as she helped them split beams apart as though they were ice. I watched as they covered rooms in vines like they were patterns on the wallpaper.

Early one morning, I followed the sound of glass tinkling into water, and I found them at the indoor pool. They were scraping glass tiles off the walls, like they had been the night Embry first saw them here.

The room was enormous. The water looked more like a small sea than a pool. I probably could have gone in without Lola or Embry's sisters even noticing. But I stayed just outside the threshold. They were tearing away the deep blue and gold in a way so reckless and focused that I didn't want to intrude. It was like my sister was letting all the screaming out of her own heart.

Lola looked my way, as though she'd sensed me watching. She paused, letting gold and blue fall from her hands.

Before I could draw back from the doorway, Lola came toward me. She grabbed my arm and led me toward a stretch of intact glass. I still felt like I was intruding, even as two of the Fairfax sisters took my hands and set them against the tiled wall. Their faces were thrilled and encouraging. *Try it*, their smiles told me.

For three years, my job had been to ignore what I felt before it got in the way of what Lola and I needed. It felt dangerous to stop now.

"You're as angry as I am," Lola whispered. "You always have been. Why do you want to pretend you're not?"

My hands wouldn't do it. It seemed more likely that I would destroy our world than a wall of glass tiles.

Lola guided my hands, setting my fingers around the polished pieces. Her hands pressed my palms against the tiles, and that was when I felt it, the rage Lola and I carried together. We'd each been holding on to it alone, but it was something we shared as much as our name and our blood.

I could not change the things the world hated in me, but my hands could rip apart these glittering walls. I could not get back what Lola and I had lost, but my hands could help break The Coterie into pieces.

My hands now carried what Lola had already known. Sometimes the only thing more beautiful than building something was tearing something down.

LOLA

WHILE WE BROKE The Coterie apart, Embry Fairfax sold off the pieces.

He sold antique vases and corbels, fused-glass lamps, legions of dining chairs. He sold porcelain caryatid lamps, a sculpture of Galatea on a dolphin, reliefs of Hercules and Hebe, billiard tables upholstered in light blue.

He quietly sent the proceeds to The Coterie's former staff and to the families of workers whose deaths his father had caused. He did not tell me this. I went through his papers while he was sleeping. He slept better now.

What happened next happened a little at a time. Lisandro and I ran jobs using the Magnificent Karina's reputation, and whenever we found anyone like us who didn't know where they fit, we invited them back here. We did it quietly, tapping them on their shoulders, whispering at their backs.

Many didn't answer. Some did. They came here with their worn-out hearts feeling older than the rest of their bodies. They came with hands that knew how to do things. They came with stories, and sometimes they told us their stories before they told us what names we should call them.

They built it back differently, this place I'd wanted to destroy. Embry was with them as they converted fountains and pools into cisterns to collect rain. Lisandro was with them as they shored up the walls, taking their time, no one rushing them like our father had been rushed. Hayden was with them as they took over the greenhouses; they planted vegetables and green herbs where there had once been orchids and lilies for cut-flower arrangements.

Before I knew it, I was alongside them. I was painting and plastering. I was kneading dough in the kitchens. I was filling flowerbeds with squash and winter lettuce.

During the day, we all worked at turning The Coterie into something else. At night, we turned it glittering and gay and radiant. We played music on the Victrolas, their brass horns like enormous morning glories grown from our dreams. We wore clothes left behind—apple-green velvet and sky-blue satin, evening frock coats and lavender trousers.

We lit our world with fairy lights. We wrote our rules in lipstick. We frightened away industry barons and heiresses with how queer we were and how hard we loved and how fearlessly we told the truth.

We were furies, scaring off anyone who wanted to manifest a world where we did not exist. They knew we could turn our bodies into branches. They knew we could turn glass tiles into thousands of stars. They knew we could make universes out of everything they would never touch.

ACKNOWLEDGMENTS

This novel about transformations wouldn't exist without a few transformations of its own—from first idea all the way to the finished book you're reading—and the people who made them possible. Here, I'll name a few:

Kat Brzozowski: Can you believe this is our tenth book together? I've been grateful for every one of them, and I'm grateful for you.

Jean Feiwel, for making Feiwel & Friends a home for characters like Lisandro, Lola, Hayden, and Embry.

L. Whitt and Andreea Dumuta for this book's beautiful cover, and Elizabeth H. Clark and Mallory Grigg for the incredible art direction at MCPG.

The teams at Feiwel & Friends and Macmillan Children's Publishing Group: Emily Settle, Tatiana Merced-Zarou, Liz Szabla, Rich Deas, Teresa Ferraiolo, Dawn Ryan, Kim Waymer, Ilana Worrell, Mariam Chaduneli, Katy Miller, Kat Kopit, Celeste Cass, Lelia Mander, Sarah Chassé, Jon Yaged, Allison Verost, Jennifer Edwards, Molly Ellis, Melissa Zar, Nicole Schaefer, Jordin Streeter, Lauren Wengrovitz, Carlee Maurier, Samantha Fabbricatore, Leigh Ann Higgins, Jo Kirby, Alyssa Mauren, Avia Perez, Dominique Jenkins, Gabriella Salpeter, Ebony Lane, Kristin Dulaney, Jordan Winch, Kaitlin Loss,

Rachel Diebel, Foyinsi Adegbonmire, Asia Harden, Katy Robitzski, Amber Cortes, Amanda Barillas, Morgan Dubin, Morgan Rath, Mary Van Akin, Kelsey Marrujo, Holly West, Anna Roberto, Katie Quinn, Brittany Groves, Hana Tzou, Chantal Gersch, Mindy Rosenkrantz; Talia Sherer, Elysse Villalobos, Grace Tyler, and Alexandra Quill of Macmillan Children's School & Library; and the many more who turn stories into books and help readers find them.

Wallieke Sutton and everyone who gets the mail where it's going.

The fellow writers who were there during drafting and many rounds of revision: Nova Ren Suma, Emily X.R. Pan, Anica Mrose Rissi, Aisha Saeed, Martha Brockenbrough, Kekla Magoon, Sara Ryan, Dahlia Adler, Karen B. McCoy, Mallory Lass, and Mary Chadd.

Michael Bourret, for your guidance and support; Mike Whatnall, Lauren Abramo, Nataly Gruender, Masie Ibrahim, Gracie Freeman-Lifschutz, and the DGB team.

Readers, for bringing stories to life and giving them space in your hearts. Thank you.

ABOUT THE AUTHOR

ANNA-MARIE McLEMORE (THEY/THEM) is the author of thirteen novels, including William C. Morris YA Debut Award finalist *The Weight of Feathers*; *Blanca & Roja*, one of *Time* magazine's 100 Best Fantasy Books of All Time; Lambda Literary Awards finalist *Lakelore*; *Flawless Girls*, an ALA Rise: A Feminist Book Project selection; and National Book Award Longlist selections *When the Moon Was Ours*, *The Mirror Season*, and *Self-Made Boys: A Great Gatsby Remix*. Their adult debut, *The Influencers*, was a *People* magazine's Best Book of April 2025 and one of *The Today Show*'s Best Books of May 2025. Find them online at author.annamariemclemore.com.

Thank you for reading this Feiwel & Friends book.
The friends who made **WE COULD BE ANYONE** possible are:

Jean Feiwel, Publisher
Liz Szabla, VP, Associate Publisher
Rich Deas, Senior Creative Director
Anna Roberto, Executive Editor
Holly West, Senior Editor
Kat Brzozowski, Senior Editor
Emily Settle, Senior Editor
Dawn Ryan, Executive Managing Editor
Kim Waymer, Senior Production Manager
Foyinsi Adegbonmire, Editor
Rachel Diebel, Editor
Brittany Groves, Assistant Editor
L. Whitt, Designer
Ilana Worrell, Senior Production Editor
Mariam Chaduneli, Production Editorial Assistant

Follow us on Facebook or visit us online at fiercereads.com.
Our books are friends for life.